A *Holiday for Romance*

Unmasking Love

PEGGY BIRD

author of *Sparked by Love*

CRIMSON ROMANCE

F+W Media, Inc.

Published by
Crimson Romance
an imprint of F+W Media, Inc.
10151 Carver Road, Suite 200
Blue Ash, OH 45242. U.S.A.
www.crimsonromance.com

ISBN 10: 1-4405-7040-X
ISBN 13: 978-1-4405-7040-7
eISBN 10: 1-4405-7041-8
eISBN 13: 978-1-4405-7041-4

This is a work of fiction. Names, characters, corporations, institutions, organizations, events, or locales in this novel are either the product of the author's imagination or, if real, used fictitiously. The resemblance of any character to actual persons (living or dead) is entirely coincidental.

Cover art © iStockphoto.com/hannamonika and iStockphoto.com/PhotoEuphoria

Acknowledgments

To a long line of actual visits to the lovely town of Ashland, Oregon, I can now add months of fictional visits as I wrote this story. It's been almost as much fun as being there in person.

Chapter 1

"Do you have a minute, Greer?"

Greer Payne looked up from the boring deposition she was reviewing for a fellow deputy D.A. and smiled hopefully at Multnomah County District Attorney Jeff Wyatt, her boss. "I always have time for you, Jeff. Especially if you have something juicy for me to work on."

Her smile faded when he carefully closed the door without responding or smiling back. "The FBI report came back on the Dreier matter and I wanted to talk to you about it."

The few traces of hope that remained in her soul disappeared. "Have a seat. Can I get you coffee or something? Oh, wait, you've probably already had your coffee, haven't you? Or have you?" She knew she was babbling but couldn't seem to shut up.

"I'm fine, thanks. Don't bother. I won't be here long." He dropped a file folder on her desk. "I've excerpted the pieces of the report and the grand jury indictments I thought relevant for you to see. In a nutshell, the FBI and the grand jury concluded you didn't do anything illegal and weren't responsible for the leaks about the interagency task force. Dreier and the Russian mobsters he was working with got their information from another source."

"Can you tell me who the source was?"

"I don't think that's relevant. Suffice it to say, they determined it wasn't you."

What little pride Greer still had bubbled to the surface. "Of course it wasn't me. I might have dated the guy, but I wasn't stupid or careless enough to give him information about what was going on in this office."

"You weren't stupid—aren't stupid. But your judgment in continuing to be associated with someone everyone in the legal community knew skated close to the edge of the law ..."

She waved off the end of the sentence she had heard—and read—too many times in the past four months since her former lover had been arrested on charges of industrial espionage, kidnapping of a deputy D.A., and accessory to several murders. "I'll regret that lapse in judgment to the end of my life, believe me." She picked up the file folder he'd left on her desk. "Thank you for bringing this to me personally."

"Of course." Jeff turned to leave, then stopped and faced her again. "One more thing. For the time being, and for I'm not sure how long, what happened is going to be, shall we say, career-limiting for you. I'll be keeping you under wraps so some journalist doesn't revive what happened a few months ago when you're prosecuting a case and contaminate it with bad press. That means you're going to be stuck in the office doing some pretty low-key tasks. Do you think you can handle that?"

"Do I have a choice?"

"Not if you want to continue working here, you don't."

"Then that's the answer, isn't it?"

He stared at her intently. "I don't understand what you mean by that, exactly, but I'm sure you'll let me know." He left, quietly closing the door behind him.

Greer sat stunned, not moving for what seemed like an hour but was probably only five minutes. In spite of her hopes, her exile to the Siberia of dull and unrewarding paperwork while she waited to have her name cleared wasn't going to end any time soon. It apparently didn't help that she was innocent. The downward slide of her reputation as one of the best legal minds in the D.A.'s office wasn't going to be reversed any time soon. All that was left was to answer the question Jeff asked: could she handle being pushed to the sidelines professionally for an unknown period of time because of a bad decision in her personal life?

And if she couldn't, what were her other choices? Quit the D.A.'s office for a private practice in Portland? That wasn't likely to work out. Her association with her discredited boyfriend would follow her. So … what, then? Leave Portland? That might not be a bad idea. Maybe she would be better off someplace where no one had ever heard of Paul Dreier, the Russian mob, or her taste in men. She had friends and family in California. Perhaps it was time to head south, back where she came from, to lick her wounds and regroup. Maybe, in fact, it was time for Greer Payne to simply disappear.

Because she sure as hell wasn't going to be happy sitting meekly in her office day after day watching everyone else get the good cases while she was assigned as pooper-scooper for the prize ponies in the parade.

She rummaged through her messenger bag for the business card the real estate agent had left when she'd come to see if Greer was interested in selling her condo. She picked up the phone, punched in the number and, when the call was answered, said, "Hi, this is Greer Payne. About that offer on my condo …"

* * *

A month later, Greer was roaring south on I-5 at a speed that would guarantee her one hell of a ticket if she was pulled over. But she didn't care. She was headed for California, and the faster she put this wretched state in her rearview mirror the happier she'd be. The landscape whizzed past her as, gradually, the green farms and forests of Oregon's Willamette Valley and Siskiyou Mountains began to turn to the yellow-brown hills more like the Golden State's scenery. She was almost there. She swore she could even smell California, it was that close. Excitement began to replace the tension and anger she'd been carrying around for months.

But less than thirty miles from the border, she heard a peculiar noise. It wasn't like any road noise she'd ever heard. It sounded more like it came from someplace inside the car. Panicked at first, she calmed down as it seemed to disappear when a new song started on her iPod. Relieved, she kept going. It had probably just been some odd instrumentation in the R & B she had blasting at decibel levels likely to make her deaf before the trip was over.

However, ten miles later she heard the noise again as she pulled away from a pit stop near Ashland, where she'd gotten one last tank of gas someone else had to pump. It was definitely the car, not her music.

Unwilling to believe her beloved Lexus would abandon her as most of her colleagues in Portland had, she ignored what she heard and turned toward the I-5 entrance ramp. But as she accelerated to get onto the freeway there was another weird noise, the car refused to shift into a higher gear, and the check engine light went on. She pulled over to the side of the on ramp and stopped. All she could think to do was what she did with a balky computer—she turned the ignition off, waited a few seconds, and turned it back on. The engine revved but the car didn't move. No matter what she tried, it refused to budge from its new home on the side of the road.

Fuck. One more desertion.

The tow truck arrived half an hour later, but the man from the garage couldn't get the car going either. The best he could do was offer her a ride into town after he loaded her car onto his truck. She was stuck for what he warned might be several days until they could figure out what was wrong.

She wanted to scream. So close to escaping, yet so far from succeeding. Although she shouldn't have been surprised. Being stranded in Ashland with a broken-down car went along with everything else that had gone wrong lately. There was no point in being disappointed. She just had to suck it up and live with it.

Yeah. Right. If she could convince herself to be calm about this, she'd be eligible for sainthood.

• • •

The room the woman at the visitor's center found for her was in a remodeled fifties motel that had been turned into a comfortable and beautifully appointed place to stay. The owners lived on site and had been alerted to her situation before she arrived.

"You poor thing," the woman at the front desk said as Greer filled out the registration information. "Car trouble is such a pain." She looked down at the paperwork in front of her. "Oops. Sorry. With your last name, I guess we don't make pain jokes."

Greer smiled for the first time in quite a few hours. "It's okay. I'm used to it."

"Well, the bright side of this is you'll have a chance to see Ashland. Ever been here before?"

"Yeah. Came up from California to the Shakespeare Festival every summer for years."

The woman looked at the registration form again. "You gave an Oregon address."

"I've been living in Portland for a few years, but I'm moving back to California. The visits were when I was a kid. Came here with my mother and sisters."

"If you haven't been here in a while, you might find a few things have changed. Why don't you take a walk around while we get your room ready? You can leave your luggage here. It'll be safe."

With nothing better to do until she could hole up in her motel room for the night, Greer wandered back toward town. The woman at the motel was right—some things had changed. Her mother's favorite French restaurant was gone, replaced by a newer, trendier eating establishment. The store where her older sister had always found clothes she liked was now a convenience store. And there was a new indoor theater added to the outdoor Elizabethan theater and the Bowmer indoor space.

But the bones of the town were the same. Ashland still had the comfortable feel of a small town that just happened to have at its core a world-class theater company.

It was also very much Oregon, as Greer found out when she ordered a late lunch at a restaurant near Lithia Park. In a manner usually reserved for explaining the provenance of a valuable painting or a special bottle of wine, her server assured her that the chicken salad on field greens she ordered was local and free-range.

After lunch she cruised through a few clothing stores where there were end-of-season sales going on. She hadn't planned on spending money on clothes, as she faced the probability of a large car repair bill and had no job waiting for her in California. But when one shop owner lowered the price of a green dress that matched the color of Greer's eyes and that the woman said was meant for her, Greer had given in. How could she resist when the owner had been so accommodating

A couple more pleasant encounters with the shop owners and residents of Ashland later, Greer realized, as she walked back to her motel, that for the first time in months she was beginning to feel relaxed—in spite of the car breakdown, the unknown cost of repairs, and the forced change of plans. Her good mood might be a reaction to the beautiful autumn day—she was walking ankle-deep in colorful fallen leaves past shop windows that were beginning to be dressed for Halloween. The air was crisp and clean, the sun warm on her face.

Or maybe it wasn't the warmth of the sun that had relaxed her, but the warmth of the people she'd met. For a town overrun with tourists for most of the year, Ashland was remarkably friendly. *Maybe*, she thought, *it wouldn't be so bad to be stuck here for a few days. I can hang out, relax, get my car repaired, and be back on the road in a day or two feeling a little less stressed and ready to face whatever's next.*

That thought held until the next morning when she called the garage. The conversation started with the mechanic saying, "We've discovered what's wrong with your car, Ms. Payne."

"Great. How much will it cost, and how long will it take to fix it?"

"Minimum cost is a couple thousand dollars. And it'll take four or five days, maybe longer, to get it repaired."

"Ouch. What costs that much and takes so long?"

"Your transmission's shot. And, unless we can find one in a shop nearby, we have to order a new one. It'll take a few days to get here. I'm sorry I don't have better news for you."

"How's it shipped, slow boat from Tokyo?"

The mechanic snorted. "If we need to order it, it'll be FedEx from Canada, actually. We'll start tracking a tranny down as soon as you come in and sign a work order."

With no other choice, Greer signed the papers, extended her stay at the motel, and began what felt like a hospital vigil waiting for her sick car to come through surgery.

By day five, with no end to her stay in sight, Greer was about out of patience. She was also out of things to divert her from worrying about the cost of this forced "vacation." The charm of having the Starbucks barista know what she would order as soon as she walked in every morning had worn off. As had the welcome she got from the employees at Bloomsbury Books, all of whom greeted her by name each time she picked up the morning paper.

Then just when she thought nothing good could possibly happen to her ever again, her luck turned.

She was settled at a table with her paper in Brothers', her favorite breakfast place, when she overhead a conversation between two men she'd often seen in Starbucks and around town. She'd figured out they were attorneys from the conversations she'd heard before and had often eavesdropped just to hear the professional chitchat they engaged in—the kind of banter between legal colleagues she missed. Today, however, it was more than just chitchat.

"Did you see in the paper that Wilson Montgomery's moving to Arizona?" the younger man asked.

"No, that's a surprise. I thought he'd be in the legislature until he was wheeled out of the House chamber on a gurney." His companion laughed.

"Apparently not. He's closing his law practice, selling his house, and leaving town. Wants to be in a warmer climate, I guess."

"Sorry to lose him. I don't always agree with his politics, but he knows more about consumer fraud than any other lawyer for three counties. No one else has his expertise. We'll miss that."

Consumer fraud? They were talking about *her* area of expertise. She'd prosecuted more cases like that than all the rest of the deputies in Jeff's office combined. She leaned over and interrupted them. "Excuse me for eavesdropping, but I couldn't help hearing your conversation. Are you saying there might be a need in town for a lawyer with consumer fraud experience?"

"Yeah, you know one?" the younger man asked.

"I may," she replied.

"If you do, there's a law practice just begging to be taken over."

"Who would I contact? I mean, if I knew someone, a friend maybe, who was interested."

The older man cocked his head and smirked. "If you're seriously interested—or your *friend* is—call Wilson Montgomery." He pulled a business card out of his jacket pocket and wrote something on the back of it. "Here's the phone number." He started to hand it to her then pulled it back. "You a lawyer?"

"Yes, I am."

"Member of the Oregon bar?"

"Yup."

"Interesting. Never recruited an attorney in a restaurant before."

"You may still not have."

He barked out a laugh. "Yeah, right." Handing her the business card he said, "I'm Jim Foster. This is George Ross. And you're …?"

"Julie Payne."

She'd replied without thinking and was so stunned at her response that she was sure she looked relieved when the man merely said, "Nice to meet you, Julie Payne. Hope we see you again." She said nothing more as the two of them rose from their table and left after a brief conversation with the restaurant owner.

Julie Payne? Where the hell had that come from? Well, okay. She knew where it had come from. But she sure didn't know *why* it had come out in the course of that particular conversation. On the drive from Portland, she'd toyed with the idea of killing off Greer Payne and resurrecting her childhood name, but she hadn't thought more about it since she'd been in town.

Her whole, legal birth name was Juliet Greerson Payne. Her family called her Juliet, a name she'd dumped in high school when she'd gotten tired of *Romeo and Juliet* jokes. She'd chosen Greer, a version of her middle name, which was the family name of her beloved grandparents. No one in her family ever called her Greer, but everyone else had, from high school on.

This morning, she'd changed all that by introducing herself as Julie. She could be Julie if she stayed in Ashland. If she had the nerve to follow up on that conversation and call the guy who was leaving town.

It had some appeal. God knows she liked the feel of the town. She'd been made to feel at home by everyone she'd met, from the tow truck driver up to and including the two lawyers she'd just talked to, since the first moment she'd arrived in town. It wasn't as if she knew what her plans were when she got to California. She'd done some online job searching while she'd been hanging around waiting for her car, but she hadn't found anything that had caught her fancy. Not the way the conversation she'd just overheard had.

Even if she found something right away in California, she'd have limited usefulness as a practicing attorney until the following year when she could take the bar exam. She'd be able to get right to work in Oregon, where she was already a member of the bar.

With the obscene amount of money she'd gotten from the sale of her overpriced waterfront condo in Portland and what she knew she could get out of her Public Employees Retirement System account, she could probably buy into an existing law practice as well as purchase a house in Ashland. Who knew what she could buy in the expensive California market?

Even changing her name wouldn't be a problem—her college and law school diplomas as well as her bar membership, hell, even the credit card she'd used to check into her motel, were all in her full, legal name.

A new job. A new life. Wasn't that what she'd been running to? She might be able to have it all by staying right where she was. All she had to do was make a phone call and see what was out there. She looked at the business card in her hand and made a decision. She'd do it. Julie Payne would make that call. The hell with Greer and the problems she'd left behind in Portland.

Chapter 2

One year later

"So, what're you planning to do to celebrate your anniversary, Julie?" Heather Branson asked.

"What anniversary would that be?" Julie asked her paralegal.

"You've been in Ashland a year this month. Don't you want to celebrate?"

Julie thought about it for a moment. "You know, you're right. I should."

"How about a party? It would be fun, and it would be good for your practice, too. You could invite business people. Maybe some of the local government folks." Heather got a sneaky look on her face. "I know a few men you should include. You know, just to make the party interesting."

"Your matchmaking hasn't worked any other time you've tried it. Why do you think it would work now?"

"Because I thought I was being more subtle this time." Heather sighed. "I don't understand you, Julie. You're beautiful. You're smart. You've been successful in establishing yourself in town. You could probably have any man you wanted. But you've turned down anyone who's asked you out. No one seems to interest you. Are you sure …?"

"I'm sure I don't need your help fixing me up, but thanks."

"Actually, I was going to say are you sure …?" Heather paused, dropped her eyes, and shuffled a few papers on her desk. "I mean, there's nothing wrong with it if you are."

Julie laughed at her assistant's reticence. "I'm quite sure I'm not a lesbian, in spite of the rumors, if that's what you're asking."

"It's just that, if you are, I know a couple women you'd like."

"Heather, you're a fabulous paralegal and you've been a good friend. Can we leave it there and not move into the matchmaking arena?"

"I just hate to see someone like you lonely."

"I'm not lonely. I have tons of friends and a full life. I like being by myself." Julie frowned slightly. "But the idea of a party isn't a bad one. How about a costume party? For Halloween."

"OMG! That's fabulous! Halloween's on a Friday this year. You could have the party right before the annual parade, and then everyone could go watch. Or take part. Whatever. Your house is pretty close to the parade route. It would be perfect."

"That's it. Find out the exact time of the parade. Put together a list of who you think I should invite, and we'll get this puppy going."

"Don't forget a costume."

"That should be easy in this town," Julie said.

"I think I'll be Wonder Woman. What do you think you'll dress as?"

"That's easy, too. Juliet, of course."

• • •

Julie spent the rest of the day as she did most days—in client meetings and writing up documents for clients who were, for the most part, nice people. After spending almost ten years dealing with the scum of the earth in the prosecutor's office of a largish city, she'd almost forgotten that the legal system wasn't only concerned with nailing bad guys. Practicing civil law for the first time in her career, she had clients who needed lawyers for reasons having nothing to do with criminal law. Clients who were usually grateful for her help and pleasant to deal with.

In the year since she'd moved to Ashland, she'd written wills and small business contracts, and handled a few negotiations between angry neighbors. But the bulk of her work had used her expertise in consumer fraud to assist individuals or business owners who were being scammed. She'd even taught classes at senior centers and retirement complexes on how to avoid being a victim.

For fun, in her free time, she'd done pro bono work for several small local theater groups. Since she was no actor, it was how she had been able to become involved to some small extent in the vibrant theater scene in town. She didn't know everyone in the theater community, but she was pretty sure that because of her pro bono work doing the paperwork for applying for 501 (c) (3) tax status or contract and copyright issues, she'd have a good turnout of well-costumed actors if she had a Halloween party.

The more she thought about it, the more she agreed with Heather. Deciding to stay in Ashland had been the best decision she'd made in—well, maybe in forever. It was well worth celebrating. Not only had she built a great new life, but she'd reconnected with a part of herself she hadn't paid much attention to in a long time: the Julie part.

Not that she'd turned into a completely different person. Julie was book-smart, just like Greer had been. It would have been hard to ignore years of off-the-charts standardized tests, perfect grades, and professional successes. And what Julie saw in the mirror hadn't changed. Like Greer, Julie was an attractive woman.

But what Julie had lost was Greer's hubris. For years, being smart and beautiful had convinced Greer she was invincible, entitled even. Nothing could go wrong in her life. A federal investigation into her personal relationship with Paul Dreier had disabused her of that belief.

She had always been attracted to handsome men with an edge to them, in college even some outright bad boys. Sometimes it was part of the attraction. Mostly she didn't care about their reputations. She was sure she could handle them. But when she came up against Paul Dreier, her lack of concern did her in. He was everything she'd thought she wanted in a man: he was good looking, a successful attorney, and well connected in the business community. Unfortunately his ethics were lower than the soles of his handmade shoes.

He'd tried to use her to get information about the D.A.'s office. She'd been blind to what he'd been doing. That's what it boiled down to. She'd never suspected he was anything but interested in her and her life. After all, she was that fascinating.

Then Dreier was arrested. Her reputation took a nosedive so fast and so steep, she got the bends trying to get back up.

So, when she morphed Portland Greer into Ashland Julie, she decided to be more careful, to err in the other direction until she could figure out how to improve her evaluation of men. The result was, in the past year Julie had not gone out with any man. Not one. She missed having interesting conversations with a charming and handsome dinner companion, and she'd pretty much forgotten what sex was like. But if making a mistake was bad in a big city, it was fatal in a small town. And Julie had no intention of committing social suicide.

In spite of her dearth of a love life, she felt good about leaving behind the Greer she'd been. In this "Julie" incarnation of her life, she lived modestly in a small house with a yard full of roses and rhodies. The modern furniture she'd had in her riverfront condo had been left there. Her new home was furnished with pieces more in a shabby chic style (sans cabbage roses), which she actually liked better, but which had never seemed right for a residence full of stainless steel, marble, and granite.

Even her bedroom was different. In her oversize Portland room, she'd had abstract art on the walls; a huge, king-size bed with an elaborate metal canopy frame that almost touched the ceiling; a silk-covered duvet; and two chaises. She'd left it all in Portland and bought a double bed with a white, wrought-iron headboard for her new home. The curtains were white; so were the linens. Every night when she went to bed, she saw surroundings reinforcing the changes she'd made—confirming for herself that the woman who'd slept with the wrong man was no more.

Although she was without a love life, she had a full social life. She hung out with people from the legal and business communities. She had friends in the local theater crowd. But she made sure everyone knew she wasn't in the market for anything more than a bit of fun. Heather was right: Julie fobbed off all offers of a date with light refusals. She'd apparently done it without offending anyone, because no one seemed annoyed with her for turning him down.

Heather's intimation was also right: there were whispers about her being a closet lesbian. She ignored them along with the rumors that she had a lover stashed away someplace. She didn't care what people said as long as no one found out what had happened in Portland. And, on that score, so far, so good.

There really was a lot to celebrate. A party would be the perfect way to mark the occasion.

Over the next week, she and Heather made a list of names and sent out dozens of invitations to business contacts, her theater buddies, legal and political colleagues, her neighbors. The invitations urged people to bring a friend or two so the event would be a way not only to mark her first year in town, but also to expand her social circle.

Heather located a Juliet costume for her: a batiste nightdress worn for the balcony scene in a local production of *Romeo and Juliet*, complete with a dark wig with a single long braid to cover Julie's very blonde and totally un-Juliet hairstyle. A white, feathered mask trimmed in gold completed the costume.

The wig came with a promise from the wigmaker to secure it so it wouldn't fall off during the course of the evening. The belt-and-suspenders approach he would take included the professional tape he normally used to secure wigs onto his actors, as well as spirit gum to make sure the skullcap stayed in place. Last, he'd tie a headband around her forehead. He teased her that the wig wouldn't come off until Thanksgiving.

A caterer was hired and the menu set. The week before the party, Heather helped Julie carve pumpkins and string twinkle lights. The day of the party, Julie set out dozens of candles around the room to create the appropriate mood. Through it all, her anticipation grew as she became more excited about celebrating what was beginning to feel like her real birthday; the day when, out of the ashes of Greer's life, Julie had been born.

Chapter 3

Trace Watkins yawned, rolled his shoulders back a couple times, and turned up the music. The dramatic end to the Beethoven symphony would, he hoped, keep him awake for a few more miles. A complication with a customer he'd been working with for weeks had prevented him from leaving Portland as early as he'd wanted. Now, some five hours after the end of his already long day, he and his CRV were almost to the Ashland exit. It meant he would get to his destination before midnight. Barely before, but still … Although Fred Arnett, his old fraternity brother, had told him not to worry about when he arrived, Trace didn't want to impose any more than he already would be.

He'd booked a motel room for most of his stay in Ashland, but they hadn't had a vacancy on his arrival night, so Fred had offered to put him up. Actually, Fred had offered to put Trace up for the three days he'd be in town. However, Trace didn't want to take advantage of someone who'd become essentially a stranger in the twelve years that had passed since they'd graduated.

Fred had visited Portland a few times, usually to go to the theater and to call Trace for dinner but Trace had never gone to Ashland. Not that Fred hadn't tried to get him there, but something always seemed to stand in the way of making the trip south. Now Trace regretted not keeping in closer touch with the man who'd been such a good friend.

The directions to Fred's house were easy enough to follow. It was near the university. After he pulled into the driveway, Trace sat for a moment or two and looked around. Even in the dark, he liked what he saw—a well-established neighborhood with Victorian and Craftsman homes, big, old trees, and shrubs. It looked welcoming. Comfortable. Like a small town should.

His friend met him at the door before he could knock. "Hey, bro, welcome to Ashland. It's about damn time you came for a visit."

"Thank you for letting me stay here." Trace extended his hand for a handshake.

"Still the same Mister Serious, I see. After all these years, a stranger's handshake?" Fred asked. "No way. You get this, not a handshake." He pulled Trace into a bear hug accompanied by a clap on the back. In about two seconds Trace hugged him back with his one free arm. Fred had always been a force of nature and, in the face of it, Trace had always given in.

Fred grabbed the suit bag and small roller case Trace had brought with him and waved his houseguest into the living room, setting the luggage on the steps to the upper floor. Trace followed, a smile on his face as he realized that if he hadn't changed much since college, neither had his friend. And he was damn glad of it.

"Of course I'm serious. I'm a banker, for God's sake," Trace said. "I don't run a theater company in paradise like you do. I handle people's money."

"You were like that before the bank hired you. If you were a carpenter, you'd measure *five* times before you even thought about picking up the damn saw, let alone using it. Good thing I don't have to worry about stuff like you do. I don't have any money of my own, and the theater's more interested in my artistic vision than my financial one. Nothing serious there." He shrugged, as if it were no big deal.

Trace raised his eyebrows in disbelief. "Well, if I take the transfer I've been offered, I'll be around here full time. Maybe I can help you figure out a way to invest what you have to make it work for you."

"You're here for a job interview? You weren't real clear on the phone." He motioned Trace into the kitchen, where he pulled out two wine glasses and held them up in a silent question.

Trace nodded an affirmative. "Not really an interview. I've already been offered the job. But before I agreed to the transfer, I wanted to see what the town's like, meet with people, get a feel for life in Ashland."

Fred poured the wine and handed one glass to Trace. "Wow. You're actually thinking about willingly leaving Portland? I thought you'd be there forever."

"I'm tired of city life. It's too smug and pretentious. I've been looking for six, eight months for something more comfortable for me, something more like where I grew up."

"Portland? Smug and pretentious? Who'd a thought?" Fred's laugh indicated he would. "So what'd Northwest Savings and Loan offer you?"

"A nice promotion—the manager's job here. The man who's here has been on the verge of retiring for a while now. Which shows in the way he's working, I guess. He's not exactly taking care of business. The powers-that-be offered him a nice golden parachute, and he took it."

"Three clichés in two sentences? Professor Georgia would be so disappointed."

"You know I only took those English classes because of the woman I was dating. I was never as fascinated by the arts as you were."

"Yet you might be moving to a place where the only games in town are theater and a university."

"Which is one of the things I need to figure out—whether I'd like living here. The job's not the issue. The banking business I already understand."

"I'd be happy to show you around," Fred offered. "I know where all the good places in town are."

"Thanks, but I'm booked solid with meetings, lunches, and dinners over the next few days."

"Then stay the weekend. The theater has a performance on Saturday night I have to attend, but I have Saturday afternoon and all day Sunday for the tour. You still a serious outdoor lover?"

"I'd like to be, but I never seem to have the time. Too busy with work." He shrugged off his lack of a personal life. "Thanks for the offer, but I should be getting back to Portland."

"For what? You got a girlfriend waiting for you?"

Trace shook his head. "No time for that either."

"Switched teams and have a boyfriend waiting, then?"

"Yeah, right." Trace took a slug of his wine to hide his smile.

"Then why do you have to get back up the freeway? Stay, and we can catch up with each other, maybe get in a hike or something. I might even pull out a surprise for you."

The opportunity to reestablish ties with his college friend appealed to Trace. If he moved to Ashland, it would be nice to have a friend not connected with his job. "Okay. You win. I'll stay."

"Good. Oh, and there's a party Friday night my girlfriend knows about. Someone from one of the smaller theater companies told her about it. I'm not sure who's throwing it, but she says it's open to anyone who wants to show up. Why don't you go with us and meet some locals? Not sure who all will be there other than a few theater people she mentioned, but free beer and something to eat sounds good to me."

"Are you sure it's okay to bring an uninvited guest?"

"We weren't formally invited either. Like I said, it's some kind of open house or something. I'm sure it's fine."

"I don't know. It doesn't sound …"

"After being stuck in Portland with the terminally hip and marginally interesting, you should try something different. Come meet some of our friends. You'll like them."

"Okay, okay." He finished off his wine. "Anything else you'd like to rearrange in my life?"

"Not at the moment, but I'm sure I'll think of something." Fred stuck the two wine glasses in the sink. "Oh, it's a costume party. You'll need something to wear other than a business suit."

"Where'm I gonna get a costume on such short notice?"

"You're in a theater town, bro. It's not a problem. I'll take care of it for you."

• • •

Slumped in the only chair in his motel room, his tie loosened and his top shirt button undone, Trace closed his eyes and tried to find one coherent thought in his mind. It took less than five seconds to confirm what he suspected—everything was gone. He had nothing left in his head.

It had been a hell of a few days. Meeting after meeting, breakfast, lunch, and dinner with bank staff, business owners, and Chamber of Commerce types, a sprinkling of university leaders, and more non-profit groups than he thought could possibly exist in a small town. At every meeting he'd had to be his best, had to be "on" at all times. What was it he'd said to Fred about the difference between banking and the theater? If he hadn't been on stage all week, making sure he came across as a reassuringly trustworthy businessman, he didn't know what he'd been doing.

Fred. Right. He'd promised he'd go to the damn costume party tonight. No way was it going to happen. Not the way he felt. He'd call his friend and beg off, then take a shower, grab something to eat from the Safeway across the street, and make it an early night.

He was digging out his cell phone, when there was a knock at his door. Who the hell? He wasn't expecting anyone.

He opened the door to a Roman soldier, complete with a dangerous-looking sword and a helmet topped with a bristly, red crest. "Brought you a costume I thought you'd like," Fred said, holding up a suit bag.

"I'm not really up to this tonight. Maybe …" Trace started.

"I knew you'd try to chicken out on your promise. So I brought reinforcements. Here's the surprise I told you about." He stepped aside to reveal another man who was dressed as if he belonged in the Independence Hall of 1776.

"Damn, Watkins. If I'd known you'd be here, I'd have stayed home. No woman's gonna look at me when you're around," the bewigged figure said.

"Kev? Where the hell did you come from, and what are you doing here?"

The Founding Father, in truth, Kevin Christopher, another fraternity brother, answered both questions in one sentence. "Came up from San Fran to see a few plays and hang out with Fred. I had hopes for scoring at this party, but now I don't know. You'll snake all the women like you always did." After he followed Fred into the motel room, he guy-hugged Trace.

"Are you serious?" Trace asked. "You were the one with all the blondes hanging on you at fraternity parties. And why are you talking about picking up women? Where's Alana?"

"Probably with her new husband. You're a couple years behind in the news."

Embarrassed he'd been out of touch with his friends for so long, Trace mumbled, "Sorry, I didn't know."

"Yeah, well … we haven't been the best at keeping in touch, have we? And I didn't exactly post it in the alumni magazine." Kevin's voice trailed off, and he almost lost his smile until he seemed to shake it off. "Anyway, it's old news. Get thee into this outfit Fred found for you, and let's go. It'll be like old times again. The three of us on the hunt. Women of Ashland beware."

"He's got a date," Trace said, pointing to Fred, "and I've had a long week. I was thinking maybe I'd have a quiet dinner and …"

"Fuck that shit. Get your ass into this costume, and let's go. Fred's date means there'll be more women for us. Let's get to it."

Fred was grinning. Kevin was smirking. Trace was apparently going to the party. He grabbed the garment bag Fred was holding. "All right. For an hour or two. Then I'm coming back here." He glared at his two buddies. "I'll change in the bathroom. I'm not stripping while the two of you watch and point."

"Oh, hell, Watkins, and here I was hoping. I haven't seen a good package like yours since the fraternity house at UNM."

"Jesus, Kev, you're still a perv, aren't you?"

"Hell, yes, and proud of it."

Trace slammed the door to the bathroom, pretending he didn't hear the guffaws from his college friends.

He opened the bag and flinched. The tights, the buckles for his shoes, the snug fitting doublet with slashed sleeves, and the soft velvet hat with a feather swooping down the side all screamed only one name: Romeo. The only thing worse would have been a Shylock costume, which Trace had been worried Fred would find for him. He stared at the costume for a few moments before yanking off his tie and pulling his shirt out of his pants. The least he could do was try it on. Maybe it wouldn't be too bad. He had made a commitment to his friend, after all, and he always kept his commitments.

When he was fully costumed, he looked at himself in the bathroom mirror. It wasn't as bad as he'd thought it would be. It was worse.

Oh, the costume fit, all right. Fit too damn well in all the wrong places. This was hardly the image he wanted to project to people he didn't know but who he hoped would let him handle their money. Commitment or not, he wasn't going out in public wearing something that left nothing to the imagination from the waist down.

He threw open the door and growled at his friend. "What the fuck were you thinking, Arnett, when you picked this out for me? Or were you thinking at all?"

Fred said, "It looks great. It fits perfectly. I had to guess at your sizes, but I think I got it just right."

"You got fuck-all right. You can't really expect me to wear this in public in front of a bunch of strangers?"

"You're insulting a very fine costume designer I know who was quite pleased with what she did for *Romeo and Juliet*. Besides, you look outstanding in it."

Kevin looked up and down Trace's body. "Oh, good, you stuffed a sock in your tights. That should draw the ladies. I'll stand beside you, latch onto your rejects, and we'll for sure need these condoms I picked up this afternoon." He offered a handful of his purchase to Trace who wouldn't take them. Kev threw them onto the table between the two beds.

The condoms were the last straw. "This is not happening. We're not in college. I'm a banker, for crissake, about to start a new job in a small town, not a teenager out to score. You guys go without me. I'll give you back the costume …" Trace turned for the bathroom, but Fred grabbed his arm.

"Don't let Kev's needling get to you. You look great in the costume. Besides, no one in Ashland knows you."

"But I want them to know me—as a reliable banker, not someone looking like he's out to get laid. How will anyone in town ever take me seriously if I parade around in this … this … getup?"

"Getup? Does anyone under the age of sixty use that word? You really have turned into a stodgy old banker, haven't you, buddy?" Kevin said.

"Back off, Kev," Fred said. "Trace, don't worry about the costume. Everyone in Ashland celebrates Halloween in a big way. The mayor was Carmen Miranda last year, for God's sake."

"Maybe she …"

"He. The mayor's a 'he.' *He* dressed as Carman Miranda."

"Still, is this the way I want to be introduced to Ashland?"

"That's why I have this for you." Fred handed him a black cloth mask large enough to cover his face from the nose up to his hairline. "No one will know who you are unless you want them to."

Trace looked at the two men who'd been his best friends for four years. They'd seen each other through drunken nights and hung-over mornings, a pregnancy scare with Kev's then girlfriend, now ex-wife, numerous academic successes, and, eventually, offers of their dream jobs. Trace had almost forgotten how much he'd enjoyed their friendship and what they'd meant to him. He'd never had friends like them, before or since. All the business colleagues in the world couldn't replace these two men.

Ever since college, he'd led a careful, organized, and terribly ordinary life. Like he told Fred, he was a banker. He followed the rules. Did what he was supposed to do. Maybe he was overdue for a little fun. Maybe it was time to do something other than what was expected of him. What would it hurt for one night to try and recreate what they'd had in college, when they were less encumbered with the weight of expectations? In this costume and with the mask, even if the people he'd met with all week were at the party, they wouldn't recognize him.

He took the mask Fred was holding out to him and tied the strings around his head. "What the hell? I'm here. I'm in this stupid suit. I might as well go to the damn party."

Chapter 4

Julie was reasonably sure there were more people crammed into her living room, dining room, and kitchen than the number she'd expected from the RSVPs. Dozens of people laughing, flirting, having conversations about the future of the theater, who should run for mayor, and God knows what else, drowned out the carefully chosen background music. Most of the catered food had disappeared in the first couple hours, so she was down to crackers, chips, the remains of a wheel of brie, and a few lonely olives, carrots, and celery stalks on the dining room table. However, since the wine and beer were holding out, no one seemed to object. Her first party in Ashland appeared to be a success.

She should have been smugly satisfied. Instead she couldn't shake the sense there was something going on, something more to the evening than friends, food, booze, and good conversation. The atmosphere felt charged. Not some scary the-dead-walking-the-earth-on-Halloween feeling, but something exciting in a good way. The energy in the crowd gave her goose bumps. She tried to talk herself down with reminders of what a practical person she was, a lawyer, for God's sake. She didn't believe in woo-woo or spirits. The only thing in the house right now was half the population of Ashland, Oregon.

But she couldn't get it out of her mind. There was something going on. She scanned the room, trying to figure it out. All she could see was a mind-boggling array of people in fabulous costumes, no two dressed alike. There was, for instance, only one Queen Elizabeth, one Princess Leia. One Santa Claus, one Napoleon. One Easter and one Playboy bunny.

Could her feeling be based on something as simple as seeing the mix of time, place, and reality in what her guests were wearing?

The time warp of a NASA astronaut chatting up an Elizabethan woman? The clash of cultures as a belly dancer walked in with her Puritan date?

Maybe that was it. Maybe it was just the comfortable way everyone seemed to inhabit a different persona for the evening. Well, except for the guy across the room, the one who looked like he'd stepped off the Elizabethan stage of the Shakespeare Festival. He seemed ill at ease in the costume, or maybe in the crowd, hanging back, not looking at anything or anybody except the bottle of beer in his hand. She should probably go make him feel at home. He was her guest, after all, even if she had no idea who he was.

But then, he wasn't the only one of her guests she couldn't identify. Thanks to the masks and costumes, few people were immediately recognizable. Unless she heard a familiar voice or someone gave her a name, she wasn't sure who she knew and who had come as the guest of a guest. Part of the reason for the party had been for her to meet new people, although she hadn't yet figured out how she planned to recognize the new people who'd come to the party unless the next time she saw them they were still in dressed in character and wearing masks.

The guy in the Elizabethan costume had arrived with a woman and two men about twenty minutes earlier. Julie thought the woman might be Amber Lake, a member of one of the theater companies she'd given some minor, pro bono legal advice to. Amber had played Helen of Troy in a recent production at the theater, and the woman was dressed in Helen's costume. Her long hair was in an elaborate up-do woven through with gold ribbon, and she wore a simple gold mask. The man in the Roman centurion costume, who Julie didn't think she knew, seemed to be her date. At first, Julie thought the other two men might be a couple, but when the guy in the George Washington suit hit on the half-drunk woman in the fortuneteller costume, it became obvious they weren't.

For some reason, she was happy the Elizabethan hunk wasn't paired up. She didn't know why he fascinated her. It was more than his looks—what she could see of them with his mask on—it was something else. She didn't really believe in auras any more than she believed in magic spirits. But if she did, she'd believe in his. He radiated … something. Something attractive, seductive. Could he be what was tickling the edge of her mind into thinking the night was magic?

Maybe if she watched him for a while she'd figure it out. Luckily he wasn't paying much attention to what was going on at the party, so she had a chance to inspect him without his knowledge. No question he had a great body. Tall and broad-shouldered, he had the best legs, the nicest ass, and, unless his Elizabethan costume included a codpiece, an impressive … well, if she'd forgotten what a well-equipped man looked like, he sure reminded her. If ever there was a reason to bring back men in tights, he was it.

The mask was a shame. It hid most of his face. More than the Lone Ranger job many of her guests wore, his reached up to his forehead, bridged his nose, and skimmed the top of what might be a pair of attractive cheekbones. What wasn't covered was a strong jaw and a full-lipped, sensuous mouth, eyes almost as black as the mask was, and, topping it all, hair that definitely was black, if the bits peeking out of a soft velvet cap with a large feather were any indication.

As if he could feel her watching him, he looked up from his scrutiny of his beer bottle label, and their eyes locked. He smiled and lifted the bottle in a salute to her. Dear God, his smile could melt the panties right off a girl. At least, if the way she reacted was any indication. Her mouth dried up. But other parts of her made up for it by getting moist and achy.

She started to take a step across the room to see if the jolt of electricity now circling her breasts and peaking her nipples got stronger when he got closer. But her recently cultivated cautious streak stopped her. *No, that's what Greer would have done,* a very stern voice in her head said. *You're not Greer anymore. You're Julie, and Julie doesn't do things like that. Ever. Not when you have no idea who he is or what he's like.*

She nodded to the stranger. When a woman dressed as a serving wench asked her where to find another bottle of wine, Julie went to the kitchen to fetch it. And while she was there, to get herself a glass of cold water.

...

Who the hell was the woman with the long, black hair? Whoever she was, Trace thought, she was stunning. Tall, with proud posture and a killer body. When the light was behind her, as it was now, the sweet curves of her breasts and hips showed through her almost-transparent, lace-trimmed nightgown. He wondered if she knew how much she had on display. He hoped not. If she knew, she'd move back into the crowd, away from the light. And the only direction he wanted her to move was toward him. So he could find out if there was any chance he could see more.

She glanced at him again, smiled slightly, and looked away. The mask she wore didn't hide the interest in her eyes any more than her costume hid the outlines of her body. Although both hid enough to make him want to see the rest.

Jesus, he wanted her even though he had no idea who she was. Had he ever wanted someone this way? It was like being struck with lightning. As he imagined a lightning strike would feel like, the impact of seeing her hit everyplace on his body. Except he didn't fall down. And he didn't know whether lightning would give him an erection like the one now pushing against the tights he was wearing.

He had to find out who she was. Find a way to get introduced. Maybe Fred or Amber knew her. Looking around, he saw the couple huddled, or cuddling, in a corner and made his way there. Barging into whatever they were doing, Trace tapped Amber on the shoulder and asked "Sorry to interrupt but do you know who the woman with the dark braid is? The one in the nightgown?"

Amber raised her head from Fred's shoulder and scanned the room. "You mean the one dressed as Juliet who's talking to the servant girl?"

"You're kidding. She's supposed to be Juliet?"

"Of course. I remember the costume. It's the nightgown for the balcony scene. One of the theaters did the play a couple years ago. Caused quite a sensation because the actress playing the role didn't wear anything under it." She looked again at Juliet. "Whoever she is, she doesn't seem to be wearing underwear either."

"You don't recognize her?"

"I'm not sure. Not with that mask and wig. It could be the actress who played the role but I thought she was out of town. Want me to find out?"

"Could you?"

"I'll try to find someone who knows and get back to you."

By the time he turned back to undress his Juliet more thoroughly with his eyes, she'd disappeared. Disappointed, he mingled with the crowd to see if he could find her or ask someone who she was. But he didn't know anyone and didn't have much to add to any discussion about Ashland, which made it difficult to get into a conversation long enough to ask about her.

Amber was his last hope, but when he looked for her after he thought he'd given her enough time to find a name, she and Fred seemed to have left. Not a surprise. Not from the way they'd been unable to keep their hands off each other on the way to the party and the way they'd kept to themselves once they'd gotten there. If he had to guess, he'd say they were probably on their way back to Fred's house now.

Then he realized Kevin and the fortuneteller were also among the missing, leaving Trace alone at the party less than an hour after they'd arrived. He'd given in to his friends' pressure to come to the damn party, and they'd ditched him as soon as they'd had one beer and, in Kev's case, picked up a willing woman.

All his fond memories of his buddies disappeared. Now they pissed him off. Especially since they hadn't helped him figure out where his fantasy Juliet had gone.

One more pass through the crowd, and he'd leave, too. He started toward the dining room but immediately felt like a salmon swimming upstream as he bucked the mass of people who were suddenly all moving toward the door. He hadn't a hope in hell of getting to the other rooms to look for his Juliet, not in this wave of people, which was growing bigger by the second. He saw no familiar black braid in the crowd, so he gave up his efforts and went with, rather than against, the current of people streaming out of the house, the festivities apparently now over.

The party, as he came to understand from the chatter of the guests around him, had been a prelude to a big parade headed their way along Siskiyou Boulevard. They were all winding up their evening either as the event's spectators or participants.

He reached the parade route and then stood for five minutes or so, trying to decide what to do. His friends had dumped him, the woman he'd wanted to connect with had disappeared, and the only way to find any of them was to search through a crowd of masked and costumed strangers. Easy, right?

Then he saw his buddies and their women across the street, making their way through the crowd to the curb. Fred seemed to know the people sitting there. Maybe they'd been saving a place for him. Trace waved, but neither man seemed to see him. Probably because once they settled in place, they looked more interested in the women they were with than anything else. If he could have reached the two couples, he would have told them to get a room.

A room. There was a good idea. Enough looking for Ms. Right—or, more accurately, Ms. Right Now. She was probably only some Halloween fantasy anyway. He'd been fooled by a party of strangers in elaborate costumes into thinking there was something special about the night. There was nothing special going on. It had just been a house full of people having a good time.

He had a room. And it wasn't far away. It had a shower and a bed and a place to ditch the damn costume. Now was his chance to escape and get the early night in bed he needed. He pushed his way through the crowd, apologizing every two feet or so for stepping on or in front of someone, determined to get to his motel before the parade was in full swing. He didn't have much time. The first marchers were already in front of him, the main body of the parade approaching the corner where he was standing.

He was looking around, trying to scope out the best time to make a run for it, when he saw his fantasy Juliet coming from the direction of the house where the party had been. She was alone and must have been among the last to leave.

Anonymous in the group of spectators, he watched her move to the edge of the crowd and stop under a streetlight, speaking to no one. She seemed as disconnected from everyone as he was. Maybe she was a stranger in town, too.

After a few moments of observing, when he was sure she was really by herself, he retraced his steps through the crowd, apologizing to the same people for the same reasons. Circling around so he approached her from behind, he walked carefully toward her, hoping she was unaware of him. When he was close to her, he slipped his arms around her waist and pulled her against his chest. "Juliet?" he whispered.

"Yes, what …?" She tried to twist in his arms, but he held her so she couldn't do more than turn her head. When she saw him, she stopped without finishing her sentence. He could feel her breathing begin to accelerate, felt her relax against him, and heard her gulp before asking, "How do you know me? Who are you?"

Without thinking, he said, "Don't you recognize Romeo?"

"No, I mean who are you really?" She tried again to face him, but he didn't want to give up the feel of her perfect tush against his erection, which had come to life again as soon as he'd smelled her perfume. He could feel, more than hear, her soft sigh as she nestled her head back against his shoulder. "I saw you at the party," she said, "but you left before I had a chance to find out who you are."

The soft underside of her breasts pressed against his arms as he tightened them around her. It was obvious she wasn't wearing a bra. Was she completely naked under the nightgown? Dear God, the thought made him even harder than he had been.

He pushed the lace at the neckline of her costume aside, intending to kiss her shoulder. What he found surprised him—a small dragonfly was tattooed at the place where her lovely neck curved into her shoulder. He gently nipped at it, then licked the spot before saying, "Does it matter who I am other than your Romeo?"

He had no idea where his boldness was coming from. Maybe it was the anonymity of the mask or the costume. Or being in a strange town on a night full of magical feelings. Maybe it was remembering what it had been like hanging out with Kev and Fred in college. Whatever it was, all he knew was he was willing to do whatever it took to have this woman who had roused such desire in him.

"No," she whispered as he continued to kiss her neck and shoulder. "It doesn't matter at all."

Chapter 5

Julie trembled at the words the mysterious man from her party whispered as he pressed his erection against her bottom. Heat from his hands seemed to burn through the thin material of her costume, making the chilly night air warm almost to tropical temperatures. And when he began to nibble the back of her neck, nipping, licking, sucking at the place where her nightgown bared some of her shoulder, it got even hotter.

She should ask him to stop. But apparently the sensible part of her had been tapped out resisting her inclination to walk across the room to him when he'd smiled at her. All that was left was the other part of her, the one that wanted him to keep going. The smell of his aftershave, his soap, something, along with the soft whisper of his voice and the feel of his arms around her, filled her senses, made her forget where she was, who she was.

She had to take control of this. Somehow. Maybe if she knew who he was under that mask. She asked, "How do you know who I am when I don't know who you are?"

"I know you're Juliet and I'm Romeo. What else matters tonight?"

Could he really not know her? Did he really think she was the Juliet of her costume, as he was the Romeo of his? He didn't look or sound familiar, although she couldn't really see much because of his mask. And he hadn't done more than whisper. Should she really believe he was a stranger in town who had been as attracted to her as she was to him from only a look across her living room?

Quietly, for her ears only, he began to recite, "But, soft! What light through yonder window breaks? It is the east, and Juliet is the sun. Arise, fair sun, and kill the envious moon, who is already sick and pale with grief, that thou, her maid, art far more fair than she."

She whispered back without thinking, "O, Romeo, Romeo! Wherefore art thou, Romeo?"

"I'm right here, beautiful." After one final kiss on her neck, he slid his hand down her arm, laced his fingers through hers, and motioned her to follow him.

Giving up any chance of finding out more, and without any thought of refusing, she did.

It wasn't until they were running across the street through the thick of the parade now in full swing that her doubts surfaced again. What the hell was she doing following an unknown man away from her house in the direction of either the Safeway or the Stratford Inn. She almost snorted at the idea he was taking her to the Safeway. Right. A man who'd pick up a masked stranger on the street was the kind of guy who'd want to get a few things to take back to the party for after the parade.

He said nothing more as they zigzagged their way through the crowd on the other side of the street and approached the motel. She should let go of his hand and return home. She didn't do things like this. Hell, even Greer had never done anything this outrageous. But the night—this man—had exerted some sort of magnetic pull on her. It had been a long time since she'd felt so mesmerized by a man. She tried to blame it on her year of enforced celibacy, but couldn't. This attraction was stronger than anything she could ever remember feeling.

No, "attraction" wasn't the right word. Need. Desire. Hunger. Thirst. Longing. She needed a thesaurus, because even those words were inadequate. It was such a powerful pull she couldn't—didn't want to—resist.

All she could do was follow him. All she *wanted* to do was follow him. She could tell herself it was because he didn't seem like someone who took no for an answer. But she knew the reason had nothing to do with him. It was all on her. She didn't want to say no. All she wanted was to get rid of the ache in her body she'd felt ever since they'd locked eyes across her living room.

Even though both she and the stranger were masked, Julie was grateful the man who was usually at the registration desk—a man she probably saw around town—was at the window looking out at what was going on in the street. He paid no attention to the two of them sweeping in and almost running down the hall. Romeo's room wasn't far away, thank God. One swipe of the key card, and they were in.

When he didn't reach for the light switch, she said, "Aren't you going to turn on the lights?"

"No," he replied, running the back of his hand over her cheek.

"How do you expect us to see in the dark?"

"There's enough light from the window, and I have great night vision. Don't you?"

"Not really." She started to remove her mask and he stopped her again.

"Keep the mask on." He threw the velvet cap onto the nearest bed. "We're going to do this my way—no lights, masks on." He reached for her. "And costume off. Now." He began to bunch up her nightgown, his hands caressing her hips as he did.

Julie had always been in charge of her own sexual satisfaction. She asked for what she wanted, made sure she got it, and, if she didn't, took care of things herself. Following orders was not how she operated. Then again, what about this night was how she operated?

If only she could see his face, read his expression. But when she reached for his mask, he grabbed her by the wrists. "Maybe I should remove temptation for a bit." He spun her around, so her back was to his front. "That should do it. Now, where was I? Oh, yes, the nightgown."

This time he didn't linger. He simply pulled her costume up and over her head and dropped it on the floor. Naked now except for a white silky thong and white ballet slippers, she resisted the impulse to cover her breasts with her hands. Somehow she knew he would tell her not to do that either. Holding her tight against him with one arm, his other hand wandered at will over her body. As his hand massaged her taut, pebbly nipples, surges of desire washed over her. He pulled at her nipples, now hard as stone yet sensitive to his touch, aching to be stroked.

"Jesus, Juliet, I don't need light to feel how soft your skin is, how beautiful your breasts are." His hand continued down her body, trailing heat over her belly, stopping at the line of her pubic hair. She moaned and tilted her hips up, urging him to continue, to end the torment and help her find release.

Instead he turned his attention to her neck, sucking, licking behind her ear in a place she didn't know could be so responsive.

"Please," she whispered, knowing how desperate she must sound, her voice raspy with want. "Please."

He ignored her and continued kissing down her neck to her spine, holding her by the hips as he progressed to her bottom, nipping at the flesh, then to her thighs. When he reached the back of her knees he lingered for a few kisses then retraced his path back to her neck. "You taste good every place." His voice was as harsh and full of desire as hers.

By this time he didn't have to hold her against him. She needed to lean on his chest to stay upright. He was now free to use both hands, and he did, turning her around, crushing her against him in a kiss that was just this side of rough. His stubble scratched against her face, a feeling she wanted in other places on her body. In every place on her body.

He dropped to his knees before her, his hands cupping her breasts. Then his mouth found one nipple, and he licked, suckled, nipped, and scraped his teeth over the now hypersensitive skin.

All of her senses were focused on one connection between them. Nothing else existed except his mouth on her. She held his head close to her body as he went from one breast to another, fueling the desire he'd aroused with his words on the street and his smile in her house.

Just when she thought she couldn't bear any further arousal, he made it even more intense by slowly, very slowly making his way down her body with hot, wet, needy kisses.

And then he was there, where the ache had been since he'd smiled at her in her living room. The ache she needed relieved soon. His tongue slicked over her sex, as his fingers parted the lips and found the nub of her clitoris. He circled it with increasing speed, and she splintered into shards of light.

She didn't know how or when it had happened, but he was standing, holding her, pressing his erection against her, kissing her hair. "I don't think I can stand up anymore," she said.

"I know how to fix that," he replied, and with one quick motion, pulled down the bed linens and lowered her onto the bed. When he'd removed her ballet flats and slipped the thong down over her legs, he began to undress himself. Without taking his eyes off her, he shed the doublet, toed off his shoes, and removed the tights. She gasped when she saw his erection. "Thought you couldn't see in the dark," he said.

"That's hard to miss." She sat up on the edge of the bed facing him and tried again for his mask. "Finish undressing. Let me see your face."

His response was the same—he gripped her wrists, tighter this time. "No, tonight is for Romeo and Juliet. Only for them." He stood, getting his face out of range of her hands. "If you want something to do with your hands, here." He wrapped one of her hands with his, guided their joined hands to his erection, and began to rub.

She looked up at him, her breathing now ratcheting up again. Saying, "I have a better idea," she shook off his hand and, continuing to massage him, began to slowly lick and suck him. First the velvety tip, then the steely shaft, then the tip again.

He groaned. "Oh, Jesus, Juliet. What are you …?" He didn't finish the sentence. His hands held her head and his hips began to move in rhythm with her mouth and hands.

She stopped when she began to sense he was on the edge of exploding and asked, "Do you have protection?"

For some reason he responded with a harsh laugh. "Yeah, a friend … never mind. On the bedside table. Over there."

• • •

While she looked for the condom, he slid into bed with her. Somehow, she'd turned his seduction of her into something he could barely control. He wasn't sure if he loved it or hated it. He was sure she was amazing. *That* he loved.

She turned back to him, and he took the condom from her, tucking it under the sheets. When he pulled her close, he could feel her heartbeat pounding under his hand, feel his own heart doing the same. She moaned and clutched at his head as he went back to kissing her breasts, using his mouth and teeth to take his pleasure, to give her pleasure, his hands molding and massaging her. He tugged at the end of her braid to bring her head back, so he could kiss her neck, her mouth, her ears. She shook her head and made a sound as if it hurt, so he let it go.

Angling her head with his hand so he had the access he needed without the masks interfering, he made the connection he wanted. Again he explored every bit of her mouth, from the graceful bow of her top lip to the lush pad of her lower one and into the corners where they met. What he had intended as a slow slide over the velvet of her tongue became a deep, hot kiss that spiraled out of his control, threatening to consume him, consume them both, from the heat of their joined mouths. As he was stealing the breath from her lungs, she was stealing the judgment from his mind until there was not enough of it or of anything else in the universe to keep him from pushing them to the next level.

Her legs parted, and he knelt between them, over her, supporting himself on his hands.

"Please," she pleaded. "Please." As if she feared he might misunderstand, she tilted her hips back to show him what she meant.

He didn't need directions.

•••

This was not real; this was a fantasy with a mysterious lover in someplace imaginary. Passionate sex with a man who seemed to know her body as well as she did, who took what he wanted from her at the same time he made her come harder and faster than she ever had before. And he wasn't finished. At least she hoped he wasn't. She needed more. Wanted him inside her so she could have another earth-shattering release.

When he kissed her again, his mouth was hot and hard as he pressed it to her, their tongues slipping and sliding in a frantic rhythm, a rhythm she wanted repeated someplace else. Tilting her hips, she tried to move so the tip of his penis was at her sex.

"You want me, don't you?" he asked.

She didn't answer but only wriggled her hips again.

"Tell me you want me inside you."

This wasn't a game she wanted to lose so she said, "You know I do."

"I want to be there. But first, I want you to come again, while I'm watching." He began to kiss her mouth. "Can you come from this?" Then, sliding his mouth down her face, he kissed her jaw, licked the outer edge of her ear and then blew softly on it.

She could feel her body shiver.

"Or from this?"

Now he moved to her neck, to the soft spot near her ear she'd never realized was so sensitive. She was finding it difficult to stay still, her back arching against him, her hips grinding into his.

"I bet this is where we can take you over the top." He'd reached her breasts and began to swirl his tongue over the nipples still sensitized from his earlier attention. The combination of his words, his erection pressing up against her clitoris, and his mouth on her breast produced another climax so strong she wasn't sure she would ever come down from it.

He held her while she came back to earth. "I didn't think it was possible, but you're even more beautiful when you come." He reached under the sheet for the condom. "Put this on me, and let's see if we can do that together this time."

• • •

She seemed exhausted from the second orgasm; he wasn't even sure she heard him when he asked her to cover him. But in seconds she had the packet open and the condom ready to put on him. He gritted his teeth when she touched him, afraid he might have been foolish to believe he could survive the pressure of her hand on him without completely losing it.

Somehow he did. When he was covered, he rested on his forearms and used his knee to separate her legs. She moved restlessly beneath him, ready for him, as ready as he was for her.

He didn't want to be rough, but the scent of her, the feel of her skin on his, the softness of her lips drove him over the edge. With one thrust he was all the way inside her. Then she wrapped her legs tightly around him, rocked her hips, and pulled him in deeper. Her body was arched against his, her head back. Their mingled sweat allowed his body to slide easily against hers. She made a soft sound in the back of her throat with each thrust. Afraid he was hurting her, he slowed down, but she whispered, "No, don't stop. Harder. Harder."

It almost undid him. He was trying to pace himself, trying to prolong the feeling of her snug channel enclosing him, but he didn't have a chance in hell to slow down. She moved under him in an increasing rhythm, her nails bit into him as she urged him on, with her body, with her words. Words like "yes" and "more" commanded him on a subconscious level, and he responded by moving faster, harder until he felt her inner muscles clamp around him, milking him as she came. He poured himself into her with only one thought: *Mine.*

She was his. For this one night, Juliet belonged once more to Romeo.

When he could make his body respond to his will, he rolled off her. He took a few minutes to suck in enough oxygen to unscramble what little was left of his brain then left the bed to get rid of the condom. That accomplished, he returned to her. She was still in the same position as she'd been when he'd left, her eyes closed, her breathing more normal.

He lay down beside her and took her hand. Neither one spoke for what seemed like an eternity. Finally she said, "I better leave."

He pulled her against his side, "No, not yet."

Her body was stiff, her attitude resistant. "I can't stay."

"I'm not asking you to stay all night. Only for a while longer." He smiled up into the dark room. "You never know. I might decide the night's not over yet."

"Bragging about your prowess?"

When he chuckled, he could feel her body relax a little. "Not really. But a guy can hope."

"Okay. I'll stay for a little while."

He closed his eyes for a moment, only a moment, to appreciate his luck in having this woman in his bed.

Chapter 6

Julie had hoped that by telling him she would stay, he would relax and fall asleep. It seemed to be working. His breathing had become shallow and regular. Now he was snoring softly. This was her chance to slip away, to avoid complications or awkwardness. If she didn't leave now, she might give into whatever part of her, or part of him, was tempting her to stay. But she knew she couldn't— shouldn't—stay and face daylight, the stranger in the mask, and all the people who would see her when she left the motel. It was simply not a rational option.

As if anything tonight with this man had been sensible.

Easing her way out of his embrace, she had a moment of panic when her braid caught under his arm. If she could have pulled the damn wig off she would have, but her friend's belt-and-suspenders approach was working only too well. After what seemed like an eternity, she eased the braid away from him and slid off the bed.

Fumbling around in the darkened room, she found her shoes, her thong, and the costume. She had a second fright when tugging and pulling failed to get the nightgown over her head, caught on the mask she'd forgotten to remove. When she yanked the mask off, the dress slipped smoothly down her body.

She sat on the unoccupied bed and put on her ballet flats. Then she took one last look at the stranger who now knew her better than most of the men she'd been with for months. He was sprawled across the bed opposite her, his gorgeous body in stark relief against the white of the sheets, his face darkened more by the mask than the lack of light. One last look became the temptation of take off the mask and finally see his face.

He seemed to be sleeping soundly. She inched carefully to the other bed, making sure not to trip on the corner of the bedspread, which had slid onto the floor. Her hand was shaking as she reached for his face, touched the mask, and began to lift it.

Then he moved. She pulled her hand back as he swatted at her as if she were a bothersome insect. Another panic moment.

It didn't matter what he looked like or who he was anyway. What was done was done. She backpedaled to the door, waiting to make sure he was settled again before opening it. Now all she had to do was get out of the motel and home without anyone seeing her.

Another panic attack occurred when she got to her house and couldn't find the house key she'd pinned into the thick, lacy border on her sleeve. Relief had her breathing normally again when she realized it wasn't missing; she was looking in the wrong sleeve. Finally, safe in her living room, she sagged onto the couch. She was home free. Time to get out of the costume and get back to being Julie.

The first thing that had to go was the wig, which wasn't easy. It hurt like hell to pull it off, and she was sure some of her own hair and maybe even some skin went with it. But when it was gone she began to feel more like herself.

Ignoring the party detritus scattered everywhere on the first floor, she headed upstairs. She wanted to strip off the costume, leave Juliet behind, and scrub away her sins in a flood of hot water and scented soap. Maybe if she took a long enough shower she could rinse away the guilt she felt about her foolish, careless, and potentially dangerous behavior. Behavior that had nevertheless resulted in the most unforgettable night of her life.

She tried, letting the hot water run over her until it began to get chilly, but it didn't work. There wasn't enough water in Ashland to wash away what she'd done. She turned the shower off before she got too cold and toweled herself dry. Once in clean pajamas, she pulled down the quilt on her bed. Sleep. Perhaps sleep would help.

As she crawled into bed she noticed the Juliet costume and wig in a heap on the bedroom floor where she'd dropped them. More guilt. She shouldn't treat such a lovely costume so badly. Her behavior wasn't the poor nightgown's fault. It shouldn't suffer because of her.

Getting out of bed, she did her best to smooth the now-messy wig. She'd have to come up with a story for her friend about exactly why it looked the way it did. She certainly couldn't tell him it was from a night of hot sex.

But it turned out that wasn't the only problem. "Everything" wasn't there. She was missing the mask. After searching her bedroom and the living room downstairs where she'd ripped off her wig, she remembered pulling the mask off so she could get dressed.

The last panic attack of the evening occurred when she realized her mask was still in Romeo's motel room.

• • •

The sound of the alarm on his phone wakened Trace at six, as it usually did. But it wasn't a usual morning. For starters, there was something over his face blocking out the light, almost like a blindfold. It took a few seconds to realize the stupid mask he'd worn the night before was covering his eyes. For a few more seconds he was puzzled at why the hell he still had the mask on, when he could feel he was otherwise naked.

Then he remembered. He ripped off the mask, hoping he'd find Juliet sleeping peacefully at his side. Of course he didn't. Like an idiot, he'd fallen asleep, and she'd left. The pillow and the place where she'd been were cold. It had been awhile since her luscious body had warmed the other side of the bed.

He closed his eyes, and images of her played like a PowerPoint presentation in his head. The way her eyes glowed when he caught her watching him from across the room. The sight of her on the street, alone, under the streetlamp. Her surprise when he called her "Juliet." His surprise when he'd uncovered the secret dragonfly tattoo on her shoulder. The way she'd reacted to his intensity when he'd stripped off her costume. How beautiful she was when she came. And came. And came again.

Jesus, what had he done? This was not how he operated. He'd had his share of sex with beautiful women in a number of places and a number of ways. But usually after a few dates and always through a conventional way of being introduced. The list of what he'd done the night before for the first time was anything but conventional, although admittedly impressive.

Sex with a woman whose name he didn't know? He could check that off his bucket list. Ordering a woman around like she was his to command? That one, too. Lights out, masks on sex? He lingered over each of those items as he checked them off also. Wanting the woman even more the next morning than he had the night before? Check. A sneaking suspicion he could fall for her in the light of day and outside a bedroom? Check.

Fear he'd never see her again? Check and double check.

He'd think this through while he drove home to Portland. He had to get away from Ashland. He needed distance to make sense of it, to understand what had happened, to figure out a way to find her again.

If he packed now and left without breakfast, he could be home by noon. Except, shit, he had to return the damn Romeo costume, and he'd promised Fred he'd hike with him. He'd better show up, or Fred would know something had happened. And Fred was the last person he wanted to know about the night before. At least, until he figured it out himself. Reluctantly, he got out of bed and headed for the shower.

Twenty minutes later, he was shaved and dressed, sitting on the edge of his bed. Bent over to tie his athletic shoes, he noticed something peeking out from under the other bed. Curious, he reached for it. It was Juliet's white mask trimmed in feathers and gold glitter. Even if he hadn't seen it in his mental PowerPoint a while ago, he would have recognized it from the smell of her exotic perfume on it. If he knew who his Juliet was and where to find her, he had in his hand an excuse to see her again, to return what was hers. And maybe get back what she'd taken from him—a part of his soul he didn't know could be taken.

Or was it a part of his heart he'd lost?

Other than his mental slide show, she'd left little with him. Just the mask, the scent of her perfume, and the memory of the dragonfly tattoo on the shoulder he'd kissed when he'd held her on the street. He'd never seen her whole face or heard her voice clearly. They hadn't talked much, and when they had it had been in whispers.

Not a lot to go on to find her again. But he was determined he would.

• • •

Amber answered the door when he knocked at eight. "This is a nice surprise. Fred didn't tell me you would be here for breakfast," she said. "Come on in, coffee's about ready." She stepped back and motioned him in. "Did you have a good time at the party last night? We kinda lost track of you when everyone went out for the parade."

"I … uh … yeah, I enjoyed the party. Didn't stay around for the parade. I went back to my room early. It's been a busy week for me, and I was tired." He wanted to talk about anything other than the night before. "Where should I put the costume?" He held up the garment bag he was carrying.

"Just put it anyplace. Fred'll get it back to the costume shop."

"Where is he, anyway?"

"He's in the shower. He'll be down in a minute. Speaking of the party, I'm sorry I didn't get back to you about the women dressed as Juliet. Someone said she was involved with one of the theaters in town, but I didn't get a name." She led him to the kitchen and selected two mugs from a shelf above the counter. "If I'd known whose party it was I would have tried to track down the host and ask him, but I was never introduced. A friend of a friend told me about the open invitation. Said it was a pre-parade open house. I guess you could tell that from the crowd. I think a good portion of the town was there. Did you ever meet the host?"

"No I didn't. But it's okay, not to worry." He picked up the coffee pot and filled the mugs. "Are you going hiking with us?"

"Hiking? Fred? What gave you that idea? I've never known Fred to go outside unless he was headed to another building." She sipped at the coffee. "Or to get into a car."

Trace laughed. "He promised to show me around today. Mentioned hiking even."

"His idea of a hike is to climb up the ladder to check the follow spots in the theater."

Fred appeared in the kitchen door. "I've been outed. I figured you'd stay over if I dangled hiking in front of you. But I hoped once we got talking you'd forget about it and I'd be off the hook." He dropped a kiss on Amber's forehead and took a sip from the mug of coffee she was holding. "Where did you disappear to last night, bro? We looked all over for you."

"I went back to my room early. I told you I was tired. What happened to Kev?"

"Last I knew, he was about to have his fortune told or his tea leaves read or some other clever metaphor for getting laid."

"I thought he was staying with you."

"In theory. But he's a big boy, and he has a key." Fred handed the coffee back to Amber. "Let's all go out for breakfast, and I'll tell you where I hear the good trails are. Talking about hiking is much more my speed this morning."

"Or any morning," Amber said. "Why don't you two go without me? You have a lot to catch up on, and I have some things to do to prepare for the performance tonight."

Fred kissed her on the cheek. "If you're sure."

"I am. I'll see you at the theater."

"I know a place you'll love," Fred said. "Brothers'. My favorite breakfast place in town."

"My treat," Trace said, "to thank you for your hospitality."

• • •

Julie didn't get to sleep until after two AM. Between beating herself up about doing something foolish enough to wreck her new life in Ashland and shivering with recollected passion at the night she'd had with Romeo, it was a hard sell convincing her mind to shut off. And once she'd gotten to sleep, dreams of a lover with no face and a gorgeous body made for a restless night.

In spite of her lack of sleep, she woke at her usual seven AM to a gray, rainy morning. Perfect. Between regrets and seeing the mess she had to clean up downstairs, she was definitely in a rainy-day mood. She put on a pot of coffee, cued up her pity-party playlist that hadn't gotten much air time since she'd been in Ashland, and began the cleanup she had planned to start last night after the parade.

Busying herself collecting paper plates, empty beer bottles, and crumbled napkins, she tried not to think about him … about what they'd done … what *she'd* done. But she couldn't. She saw him standing in her living room looking like an Elizabethan god. Heard his whispered commands as he stripped her naked, body and soul. Felt his hands on her body, his mouth on hers. He was a presence that wouldn't go away.

Wouldn't go away. Suppose he couldn't go away. The fear he was from Ashland floated to the surface again. Then another thought occurred. Maybe he took her to a motel because he needed to hide his identity. Maybe he was married. She'd never done anything like that, never would. Except, if he were married, wouldn't it mean he wouldn't want anyone to know what had happened any more than she did? Talk about a two-edged sword. Maybe she should try to find out who he was, to prepare herself. She remembered the room number. She could call the motel, ask who was in the room. Would they tell her? She didn't think so, but if she really wanted to know, she could try. Maybe she didn't want to know.

By the time she'd worked through all the "maybes" she could think of, she'd gotten most of the trash collected, and the coffee cups and serving plates into the dishwasher. Time for a break. She was hungry but didn't want to cook. Brothers' it was.

One look in the mirror, and she grabbed an Oregon Shakespeare Festival baseball cap and a large pair of sunglasses. They should cover the disaster the wig had made of her hair and what a night of little sleep had done to her eyes. The disguise might not be necessary—with any luck, she wouldn't see anyone at the restaurant she recognized or who made her blush. But a little bit of insurance was still a good idea.

• • •

"So, you think you'll take the job?" Fred asked after they'd ordered their breakfast.

Trace was looking around the small restaurant. Mask or not, his night with Juliet was so intense, he was sure he'd recognize her as soon as he saw her. If only he could find her before he headed back to Portland. Maybe talk to her over a cup of coffee. See if she felt the same way he did about what happened.

"Earth to Trace. You here with me or someplace else?"

"Sorry, Fred. I didn't get much sleep last night. Too wound up from the week, I guess." Trace concentrated on his water glass, hoping his friend couldn't read the truth on his face. "What were you saying?"

"I asked if you thought you'd take the job."

"I'm going to accept as soon as I get to the bank on Monday. It's a great opportunity for me, and I like what I've seen of Ashland."

Fred put up his hand for a fist bump. "All right! I'm stoked. Two of the three musketeers together again."

"One of the musketeers has to behave himself more appropriately than he did in college, or he'll lose his job because the good citizens of Ashland won't trust him with their money." *And he sure as hell better behave more appropriately than he did last night. For the same reason.*

"I'll let you in on a secret. I have to behave responsibly, too, or my board would fire my ass. And Amber wouldn't stick around if we got up to some of our college antics either."

Trace picked up something in his friend's voice that made him ask, "You want her to stick around?"

"Yeah. I think this one's a keeper. *The* keeper."

It was Trace's turn to initiate the fist bump. "Let me know when to arm wrestle Kev for the honor of being best man."

"If you're in town, you'll be the first to know."

The waiter had almost reached the table with their lattes, when a tall woman wearing jeans and a baseball cap bumped into him, causing him to dump both cups of hot coffee into Trace's lap.

"Oh, shit," Trace yelled as the hot liquid hit a particularly sensitive part of his anatomy. "Watch where you're going, will you?"

She had her hand over her mouth in an expression of horror. "I'm so sorry. I didn't mean ..."

The waiter was busy mopping up the floor and, from furtive glances at Trace's crotch, trying to figure out how to sop up the coffee there without embarrassing either of them. Fred jumped up to get more napkins.

Trace looked at the woman, who seemed to be both genuinely sorry and positively humiliated. "It was an accident. It's okay. Next time, maybe taking your sunglasses off while you're inside …?"

Still not removing the glasses, she wiped under one lens as if to rub her eye—or brush away a tear. "I apologize. Again. Your breakfast is on me. I'll leave money with the cashier."

Before he could say anything else, the woman turned, went to the front counter, handed a wad of money to the man working there, and ran out the door.

Fred returned with the napkins, which he handed to Trace. "Well, that's one way to get our breakfast paid for, I guess."

Busy blotting the coffee from his lap, Trace didn't realize his friend was still standing, looking toward the door. When he finally registered his friend wasn't paying attention to what was going on at the table, Trace asked, "Now you're off in the ozone someplace. What's going on?"

"I'm wondering who that was. She looks sorta familiar but not really, know what I mean? Like I should know her, but can't put my finger on it."

"Yeah, well, I'll pass on getting to know her any better if that means more hot coffee in my lap."

"She had a nice body," Fred said.

"I didn't notice. I was too busy having mine scalded."

Fred finally sat down, a smirk on his face. "Put you out of action for a while, did she?"

No, Trace almost said. *What will put me out of action until I find her again was last night with a beautiful raven-haired Juliet who looks like a saint and makes love like a sinner.* "Fortunately, I'm wearing jeans, which gave me a bit more protection than that costume you made me wear last night. If she'd dumped two lattes on me when I was wearing those tights, I'd have to give up on any plans to be a father some day."

•••

Julie walked away from Brothers' as if the hounds of hell were after her. Speed-walking barely began to describe the pace at which she was putting distance between herself and the scene at the restaurant.

The guy she'd spilled coffee on was right. She should have taken off her sunglasses. But she hadn't wanted anyone to see her tired, swollen eyes. She had a reputation as a reliable attorney to maintain, after all. All she'd been doing when she'd run into the waiter was looking around to see if there was anyone she recognized. Anyone who might have seen her the night before on the sidewalk, following a perfect stranger off to his motel room.

And, oh, God, was he perfect when they got there.

She had to stop thinking about it. And she had to get some food in her stomach. She was still hungry and still not interested in cooking. Greenleaf was open for breakfast. She'd go there. Then she'd go home and take a nap. That should help, too.

Food. Sleep. Not thinking about Romeo. That would take care of her problems. At least for the moment.

Chapter 7

Trace tried to forget the mysterious Juliet he'd bedded on Halloween, but he couldn't. Over the next few weeks, even while he was caught up in the details of closing out his work and personal life in Portland, he was unable to get her out of his mind. He'd wanted the job in Ashland for several reasons before their encounter, but now, close to the top of the list of reasons for moving there was the chance to find her again.

Of course, he had no idea where to start. He supposed he could go around Ashland asking all the dark-haired women to show him their shoulders so he could look for her tattoo. Or he could kiss them all and see which one sent his senses reeling. But neither action was guaranteed to find him his Juliet, and both would likely earn him a restraining order and lose him his new job.

Desperate, he took the mask she'd left in his room to the Nordstrom perfume counter and asked if they could identify her scent. Why he thought knowing the name of her perfume would help, he wasn't sure. But he did. Unfortunately, the usually helpful sales associate failed to precisely identify it. She did manage to give him more information than he ever thought possible on Oriental, amber-based perfumes, which she said was what it smelled like. She babbled on about Oriental floral, Oriental spicy, Oriental woodsy, Oriental something else before he stopped her and thanked her for trying to help.

The mask sat on his bedside table, where he could smell the gradually dissipating perfume every night when he went to bed. In his dreams, a mysterious Juliet played a starring role wearing the mask and nothing else, whispering "Please." And "More." And "Harder." He inevitably woke up frustrated with a painful erection, a dry mouth, and no one in bed with him.

Never had he been so eager to move as he was by the time he left Portland.

His belongings went into storage until he could find a place for them in Ashland. He would be staying with Fred until he did. Online he'd found a half-dozen interesting looking houses, and he spent his first weekend in his new hometown inspecting them. One stood out. He made an offer. His real estate agent told him she'd have something back for him before he closed out his initial week of work.

When he walked into the bank for his first day on the job, he felt organized and in control of what was going on.

It was not to be.

First of all, his predecessor's accumulation of personal belongings after thirty years in the same building was still in the office that should have been Trace's. Apparently, former manager Clyde Lindstrom, who'd officially left the prior week, had come in every day, sometimes taking home a box or two but making no real progress in getting the office empty. It being a small town, and Clyde Lindstrom being a well-liked local boy, no one wanted to hurt his feelings by making him move any faster at getting the stack of boxes full of framed pictures, good citizen awards, his running clothes and who knew what else out of the bank. Besides, he had to do it all himself. He had no one to help him now that his wife was gone.

Trace's new—and his predecessor's former—administrative assistant, had an embarrassed expression on her face when she showed him to a small temporary space that looked more like the place where they stored junk than a real office. It featured beat-up furniture with books holding up one leg of the desk, a computer that looked to be a Paul Allen/Bill Gates garage prototype, and a long walk to find his staff. It seemed like everyone he was introduced to apologized, swore it would be taken care of, and brought him coffee from the coffee house next door to bribe him to be happy about it

Then, he had barely settled into his cramped quarters before a steady stream of bank customers assailed him, each telling him much the same story: beginning earlier in the fall, they'd gotten phishing emails on fake bank letterhead notifying them about winning the lottery in some obscure country. Those emails had been followed by an announcement about a valuable but unnamed prize to be awarded after the winner submitted funds to cover finder's fees and shipping expenses, and provided bank account information so the money could be directly deposited.

One or two people had unfortunately responded to the offer; most had not. Nevertheless, money had disappeared from a number of accounts, ranging from $100 to $1,000, with a notice saying that now that their finder's fees and shipping costs had been paid, they'd receive their prize. Of course, nothing ever appeared. Their accounts had been hacked, their identities potentially stolen, and their money gone.

Each victim had reported it to the bank. The response from the former manager? They should open new accounts, and he'd get the situation under control. And while it was true the stream of unsanctioned withdrawals stopped as soon as the accounts were closed, they were still waiting for the bank to do something about what had already happened. And were still receiving annoying sweepstakes announcements by email on bank letterhead, no matter how they tried to unsubscribe or block them.

Between visitors, Trace searched for what his predecessor had done to take care of the problem. He couldn't find much. And his new staff wasn't any help. They knew what had happened, but they didn't know what their old boss had done to correct it.

Curiously, no one in the home office had heard about it. Trace did discover a written report from a local, outside investigator who had been hired to look at the bank's computer system. He'd reported there was nothing wrong. Trace needed time to look into it further, which didn't help him with the dozen or so conversations he had with frustrated customers over the course of the morning.

It also left him with little to say to his last visitor of the day. Customers who talked politely had come to see him first. Now the lawyer with the big stick, cold eyes, and a firm handshake made an appearance.

After the formalities were over, his visitor began, "Mister Watkins, I represent a number of people who bank with you. Their financial and personal lives have been compromised by the bank's refusal to do anything about a flawed computer security system, and we're contemplating a class action suit against the bank. I know you're new in town, but I wanted to introduce myself and let you know we're not willing to let this go on much longer. If you won't take this seriously, can't get this under control, I'll have no choice but to file suit."

He looked at the woman across the desk from him—she'd introduced herself as Julie Payne—and wished he were in the real manager's office where he could look a lot more imposing than he thought he did in this makeshift dump. With this woman, he needed all the props he could get.

She was beautiful, without question. A tall, cool blonde, she was dressed in a dark blue suit that looked like it had been tailored for her and the kind of shoes that made him wonder how women walked in them. To go by just her appearance, he'd certainly say most men would give her a second—or third—look. However the tone of her voice would drive away any man with the sense God gave rocks. It had "shark" written all over it—if you could write on voices. Which you probably could with hers, as long as you used an ice pick to do it. If ever a woman deserved to be labeled ice queen, this one did. He came close to shivering from the look she gave him as she made her case.

"Ms. Payne, you'll have to forgive me for not being able to immediately respond to your demand. I've been on the job for," he consulted his watch, "exactly seven hours and forty minutes, and until four hours ago, I'd never heard about this problem. I'm sorry you haven't gotten the response you wanted from us, but I'm going to have to ask you to be patient for a little while longer."

She pulled a business card from her messenger bag and handed it to him. "My clients can't be expected to have much patience when they're worried about having their bank accounts looted, Mister Watkins. Call me when you have some information for us." She stood and looked like she was about to leave.

Before she could, he said, "I can do better than that. I'll be in touch with you every week to let you know the progress we're making. Say, on Fridays. Or another day, if it would be better for you." He flicked the business card back and forth across his thumb, watching her as she walked to the door. She moved like someone he knew. But he couldn't put a name to the person.

She turned to answer him, but he interrupted.

"Forgive me for changing the subject, but you look familiar somehow. Have we met? It would probably have been in Portland. I just moved here, and I only know one or two people in Ashland."

"Portland? You came here from Portland?" Her icy voice now had a high-pitched tone to it. If she hadn't come into his office and taken command of the room, he would have thought she was nervous.

"I was an officer at our main branch there. I transferred here when the old manager retired and I was promoted."

"No, I'm sure we've never met." She opened the door. "Thank you for seeing me on what must be a busy day for you."

She was almost into the hall when he said, "You didn't answer my question—is Friday a good day to contact you, then?"

"Oh, right. Friday would be fine." And she was gone without making further eye contact with him.

• • •

Damn it. She'd been afraid her past would come back and bite her in the ass. And now it seemed to have happened. He recognized her. She was sure of it. When she'd lived in Portland, she'd banked at the main branch of Northwest Savings and Loan, and he'd worked there. It wasn't being vain to say men always noticed her—noticed Greer. If not her long blonde hair and big green eyes, then the body she worked hard to keep in shape. In Portland with a personal trainer, here by running every day.

She thought he looked familiar, too. She must have seen him in the Portland branch. Although for some reason, in her mental picture of him, he was in jeans, not a suit like the one he was wearing today.

What was she going to do if he confronted her? Threatened her with exposure? Was he so desperate to protect the bank that he'd use the scandal from Portland as leverage? Of course he would. He was new in his job. He'd make a big impression with his bosses if he saved them from a lawsuit. On the other hand, what kind of impression would he make on the community if he strong-armed her into backing away? God, she wished she knew if he'd recognized her. Then she'd know what to do.

She could walk away from her clients, she supposed, so they wouldn't get caught up in the mess she'd made in Portland. But it didn't seem like the right move. They'd been damaged by the bank's sloppiness and needed someone to make sure the right thing was done to correct it. And all the other lawyers around had turned them down. She didn't want to desert them. Most of the affected group consisted of students and older people who didn't have the money to fight a big, powerful bank with its high-paid attorneys.

No, she couldn't walk away, not unless she was forced to— or asked to. She'd have to keep her contacts with Mister Trace

Watkins to a minimum until they got this settled. Maybe she would be able to confine her dealings with him to email and the phone. Maybe he'd forget he recognized her.

It was too bad, really. He was certainly worth meeting with if only to admire his good looks. He had a conservative businessman style about him that was not usually her taste. But this guy was different. In another life, another time, she might even have been attracted to him. Maybe it was because the suit he was wearing didn't do much to hide a seriously buff body. His shoulders were broad and his chest hinted at being muscular. She wondered if it would feel as good to touch as Romeo's had?

No, stop. She wasn't going there. She'd managed to push Halloween out of her daytime consciousness if not out of her dreams at night. Why the hell had this guy made her think of it again?

Chapter 8

After a week in a temporary space he couldn't seriously consider an office, Trace finally lost patience and directed his staff to box up what remained of Clyde Lindstrom's belongings and put them in the temporary space so he could move into the manager's office. One problem solved.

But the more serious computer hacking issue was not as simple to take care of. Emails and phone calls to Lindstrom went unanswered, and Trace's plans to corner his predecessor when he came into the bank failed. The one or two times they'd been in the building at the same time, Lindstrom had left as soon as Trace had asked his assistant to bring his predecessor to his old office. Lindstrom always seemed to have appointments with doctors, investment advisors or, who knows, the governor.

Now as frustrated as the customers he'd talked to, Trace turned the whole problem of the hacking over to the head of IT in Portland. As promised, he reported what he'd done to the ice queen lawyer. She was not impressed. Nevertheless, now he was free to get on with what he was in Ashland to do—stop the decline of businesses banking with them and increase the number of people who used their mortgage department. The challenge was one of the reasons the job had appealed to him. It was what he did well: figuring out what worked and improving what didn't.

He met with business owners and real estate brokers. He reviewed how this branch implemented the bank's policies and procedures. He brainstormed with his staff. With the force of his personality and some positive suggestions, he began to get things at work mostly under control, where he liked things to be. It was the best beginning to a new job he'd ever had.

So, with the hacking problem in someone else's court, his strategy for improving the bank's business developing, and his house deal done, all he had left to do was to answer one question: where the hell was his Juliet?

It was driving him crazy. He was desperate enough to sit in restaurants and try to sniff out her perfume on the women who walked by. He watched every woman who came into the bank in what he thought was the correct age range to see if she recognized him. Foolish, he knew, because even if the right woman walked in, she wouldn't know him because of the mask and costume he'd been wearing. Or the nothing he'd been wearing when they'd been in his bed.

One day he even followed a woman with long black hair for two blocks until he saw how uneasy he made her—she darted into a shop and watched him from the window as he went past. That was when he realized he had to figure out something to take care of the problem before he embarrassed himself and undercut the reliable reputation he was so carefully cultivating.

The only thing he could come up with was a long shot—hunting down the host for the Halloween party so he—she—could identify Juliet. He asked Fred for help, saying he wanted to add the host to a list he was putting together for a housewarming party he was planning. Throwing a party was true. Adding the host to the list wasn't exactly true. But his friend didn't need to know that.

Fred reminded him that he'd never known who the host was. His girlfriend, Amber, who might at least know someone who knew someone who could identify the host, was on location someplace in the South Pacific for a reality show and was inaccessible.

Not anxious for Fred to get curious, Trace didn't ask his buddy any more questions. Instead, he went looking for the house where the party had been so he could find the owner. It wasn't as hard to find the house as he'd expected. Nor was it difficult to find the owner's name from public records. What he found, however, created a problem. The house belonged to the ice queen who was threatening to sue the bank. Wary of making her suspect he was trying to influence the case somehow, he dropped the only promising line of investigation as a dead end.

Then one Friday night, his staff invited him to have a beer at the Standing Stone Brewing Company where they were celebrating several recent birthdays. It seemed like a good thing to do. It turned out to be a goddamn miracle.

The crew from the bank commandeered a corner with a few tables pushed together and ordered nachos, fondue, and fries along with pitchers of the brewery's IPA and amber ale. Encouraged to shed his suit jacket and tie, Trace stood to hang the jacket on the back of his chair. Before he could sit down, a familiar shark lawyer swam past him along with a school of young, less-formally dressed men and women headed for a table close to where his group was. He wondered who they were and why they kept company with the ice queen. Not only hung out with her, but also had her laughing—indicating she possessed a side she had yet to reveal to him. It surprised him to think she would ever let go enough to enjoy something, anything.

The next surprise made the first one pale into insignificance.

As he watched, she, too, removed her suit jacket, revealing a white camisole underneath. A camisole which bared her shoulders and showed off a small tattoo of a dragonfly right where her neck curved out to meet her left shoulder.

The exact tattoo his Juliet had and in the exact same place.

He sat down with a thud, stunned. It wasn't possible. The ice queen lawyer couldn't be his Juliet. They were as unlike as chalk and cheese. Oil and water. Heat and ice.

Then he connected a few dots. "Julie" could be a nickname for "Juliet." The two names were only one letter apart. Suppose she'd picked her costume because her name really *was* Juliet? When he'd come up behind her on the street, she'd answered right away when he'd said "Juliet." And asked how he knew her.

Then there was the tattoo. He'd already noticed there were dozens, maybe hundreds of people with tattoos in Ashland. Even so, the odds of two people having the same tat in the same place were, he imagined, astronomical.

He knew she owned the house where the party had been, which meant instead of looking for a party guest, he should have been looking for the hostess. Last, her eyes were the same color as his Juliet's, although at her meeting with him at the bank, they'd been cold as stone, not glowing with desire as they'd been on Halloween.

The only dots he couldn't connect were Julie's blonde hair and the fact she didn't wear the same perfume. His Juliet had long hair, black as night, the color of a raven's wings. Julie was a blonde with shoulder-length hair, now pulled back and pinned up in a severe-looking bun. Had she bleached it?

Wait. When he'd asked Amber about her at the party, she'd described her as, "The woman in the wig and Juliet costume." Damn. He'd spent all this time looking for a woman with the wrong color hair because he'd forgotten his Juliet was wearing a wig.

As for the perfume, had he been close enough to recognize it on her when he'd met her in the crappy bank office that smelled like overripe mold?

He had to talk to her. Had to see if she wore the distinctive scent; had to see if he could jog her memory so she realized who he was.

Making an excuse for wandering off from the bank party, he approached her table. She looked up at him, her green eyes looking surprised, neither cold nor hot. "Mister Watkins. To what do we owe this honor?"

"I wanted to say hello, Juliet. I called your office today to give you the weekly update but you weren't in." He searched her face while he waited to see how she would react. She looked disconcerted, he thought. *Good. Maybe I'm getting someplace.*

"It's Julie, Mister Watkins. And I got your message, thanks."

"Julie then. And it's Trace." He took an empty seat next to her.

"You still haven't answered my question, *Trace*. What can I do for you?"

Plenty, beautiful, if you're who I think you are. But I have to shake you up again to find out.

"Like I said, I wanted to make sure you got my message. And I wondered if I could buy you a cup of coffee tomorrow so I could give you the update, and maybe we could get to know each other better while we talked about the situation."

She was shaking her head before he finished what he was saying. "I don't think so. I'm about to sue you, remember? I don't want my clients thinking I'm colluding with the bank."

"Sleeping with the enemy, in a manner of speaking?" *Let's see if she takes the bait.*

It didn't faze her. "Hardly. But thanks for the invitation." She glanced over at the table where the bank employees were sitting. "It looks like your food has arrived. Maybe you better return to your colleagues before they eat it all."

"I appreciate your looking out for me." He cocked his head and smiled at her. "Sure you won't have coffee with me tomorrow?"

"Yes, quite sure. Thanks again for asking."

"My loss. Maybe another time."

Five minutes later, just as he remembered he still hadn't given her the information he wanted relayed to her clients, she left the brewpub. He took it as a sign he'd rattled her. He wondered if she'd recognized him after all. He was more and more sure she was who he'd been looking for, although the perfume thing hadn't worked out. He didn't think she'd been wearing any perfume at all. She smelled clean and sweet, not hot and Oriental spicy, flowery, or whatever the rest of them were. Of course, maybe she didn't wear perfume when she was working.

So either he'd have to find some way to get her to admit she was his Juliet, or he'd have to see her naked and kiss her. His cock hardened at the thought. It seemed unlikely that would happen any time soon, but a guy could dream.

Then he had an idea. He had something he could use to push her into a corner and prove he was right, make her admit who she was. Once he solved the mystery of his Halloween encounter, maybe, just maybe, he'd get to confirm her identity the other way. The one involving no clothes.

• • •

Julie didn't sleep well the night after she ran into Trace Watkins. He'd irritated her. Or scared her. Or both. She wished he'd drop the other shoe, the one where he said he knew what happened in Portland and why she left the D.A.'s office. But if he knew about Portland, knew it might possibly ruin her reputation in Ashland, wouldn't he have tried to use the information by now to head off any possibility of a lawsuit against the bank? If he wasn't going to try and pressure her to back off, why did he keep dropping hints like he knew something about her?

Maybe that's what the invitation for coffee was about. Maybe it wasn't an attempt to put their relationship on a personal level in spite of getting all "Julie" and "Trace" with her. Was the purpose of the invitation to soften her up with smoldering smiles and coffee? Lull her into meeting him so he could drop the bomb, tell her what he knew and what his price was for keeping it quiet?

She had no idea what he was up to. All she knew was he was a confusing—and sexy—S.O.B.

She woke the next morning with the need to clean. It was her default activity when she was worried or under extreme pressure. Fortunately, or unfortunately, depending on whether one was concerned about her mental health or the condition of her house, since she'd moved from Portland, the urge to play maid had been minimal.

As a result, there was much to keep her busy as she made up for her previous inattention. She dusted, waxed, swept, vacuumed, polished, cleaned, scrubbed, and scoured everything she could get her hands on. Sheets and towels were washed. The oven cleaned— well, the oven turned on to clean itself. The refrigerator emptied and wiped down. She didn't stop for lunch, grabbing a leftover chicken leg at noon and a banana about two hours later.

By five o'clock she was finished. She was tired; she was hungry. Her house was spotless, and she had managed to work out the worry. A shower, clean jeans, and a turtleneck sweater later, she was about to pour a glass of wine and make dinner when the doorbell rang.

She wasn't sure who she expected to find when she opened the door, but it wasn't Trace Watkins with a smile on his face and his hands behind his back.

"Mister Watkins. What are you doing here?" Her stress levels began to climb rapidly to their pre-cleaning levels.

"I thought we'd agreed it was Trace, Juliet." His smile was so engaging. So damn sexy. So … vaguely familiar.

"And I thought we'd agreed it was Julie. Outside a few family members, no one calls me Juliet."

"I did."

"Yes, in the brewpub, where I asked you to call me Julie."

"No, I didn't mean the brewpub. I meant on Halloween."

Her hand froze on the doorknob; her breath hitched and her heart rate ratcheted up. The same sense of impending disaster she'd had in Portland the day the feds came to interview her returned in a most unpleasant déjà vu. He not only knew about Portland, he knew about Halloween?

"What about Halloween? You weren't here then." Damn it, she needed to sound in control, not like some babbling, squeaking mouse.

"Yes, I was. I was in Ashland the week of Halloween to talk about my new job here. I came to your party with my friend Fred Arnett and his date, Amber Lake."

"No. I don't believe you. Oh, God. It's not possible. No. You're making this up." She could barely get the words out, her throat was so tight. "Why are you doing this?"

He brought his hands from behind his back. In his right hand was the mask she'd worn with her Juliet costume. "This belongs to you, doesn't it?"

She recoiled from him as if snakebitten. "Where'd you get that?" she whispered.

"You left it in my motel room."

Stumbling, trying desperately not to cry, she backed into the living room, putting space between herself and the evidence of what she'd done. He followed, closing the front door behind him.

"I've been looking for you ever since I moved to Ashland." He came within arm's reach and stopped.

She snatched the mask from his hand. "Why? For more cheap sex?"

His response sounded unaccountably angry. "I certainly don't remember the night that way. Nothing we did was cheap. And it was more than sex. If you won't admit it, I will."

She fingered the elastic band on the mask, tempted to put it on, to hide behind it once again. "How did you find me?"

"I saw your tattoo last night, when you took off your jacket. I kissed that tattoo, out on the street, when I came up behind you."

An involuntary shiver from the memory of his mouth on her shoulder shook her. "But how did you know where I lived?"

"I looked for the house where the party had been held, so I could ask the host how to find you. I found the house and found out who owned it, but didn't know how to ask you about what I thought was a party guest. I didn't put all the pieces together until last night when I realized *you* were my Juliet."

His Juliet? What did he mean? "So, when I came into your office you didn't know me? Didn't recognize me from Portland?"

"Why would I know you from Portland? We'd never met until I came here."

Hope—or relief—began to flicker in her gut. "You're sure you don't remember me from Portland? I kept thinking, that day in your office …"

"The day you accosted me in my office?"

"The day I had the appointment with you. I thought I'd seen you before. And you said you thought you knew me."

"I couldn't figure it out. You seemed familiar, but you weren't who I'd been looking for. I thought I was trying to find a woman with long black hair. I should have recognized your eyes, but they weren't exactly the same when you were threatening to sue me as they were when you were …"

"Stop. Just stop." She began to pace the floor. "So, now you know. We've met."

"Is that what you call it? I think we've done more than *meet*, don't you?"

"What do you want? Money? I don't have a lot but I can see what I can put together."

"You think I want to *blackmail* you? What in hell did I do to make you think I'm that kind of man?" Now he was really sounding pissed off. "I can't think of even one reason I'd want to blackmail you."

"I can think of several. If you don't want money, then you want power. Control." She stopped in front of him. "You want to get your bank out of hot water by forcing me to persuade my clients to drop their lawsuit. If you're protecting your precious bank, you're shit out of luck. I won't back off. Tell whoever you want what I did." If she could stay mad at him, maybe she had a chance to keep from crying.

"What *we* did. I was there, too. And if I out you, I out myself, don't I?" He reached for her arm, but she eluded him. "I'm sorry you have such a poor opinion of me. I'd hoped you remembered me with a considerably different feeling."

The second time he tried to touch her, she was too slow to evade him. His hand on her arm sent a shockwave of sensation through her, every part of her suddenly remembering what it felt like to have him touch her. She closed her eyes against a powerful hunger sweeping over her, the yearning she'd been trying to tamp down, to ignore, ever since she'd walked out of his motel room. How could she make him stop touching her? If she didn't, she wasn't sure she could keep from melting into his arms and kissing him.

He went on, "I've been trying to find a way to track you down even before I got to town. I didn't know you were involved in a legal action against the bank. All I knew was I'd had the best night of my life with a mysterious woman, and I had to find her again. To see if what we had could lead to something."

"I can tell you the answer. There's nothing between us. I made a reckless mistake on Halloween. It can't lead anywhere. The town's too small. There's too much at stake."

Suddenly, he reached for her face. His touch was gentle, tender. Without thinking she leaned into his palm, pressing her cheek to his hand, sighing.

"Nothing between us? I don't think so." He ran his hand down her arm and took her hand. "Look, Juliet, have dinner with me tonight. So we can talk."

"Dinner? In Ashland? Everyone will know, will gossip."

"Let them. We have every right to have dinner together. I'm not married and I hear you're not either. For all anyone knows, we're working out a settlement agreement. Or discussing a way to protect the bank's customers."

She closed her eyes for a moment. On one hand, she wanted him to take her in his arms, kiss her, make her feel like she'd felt on Halloween. On the other, she still didn't trust him enough to believe him about why he tracked her down. He could be as damaging to her reputation here as that bastard Paul Dreier in Portland had been. She couldn't take the risk of it happening a second time because of her bad taste in men.

But she was so attracted to him. She was afraid of what she might do, of how she might give in to him. The only way to protect herself was to get him out of her house, into a public place. And since he seemed unwilling to leave until she agreed to have dinner, she'd say yes. Maybe over dinner she could think clearly enough to find out what he really wanted.

She opened her eyes and looked directly at him. "Okay. Dinner. At the brewpub."

"The pub's a little noisy for talking."

"All right, then where would *you* suggest?" Apparently he was as bossy about dinner as he had been in bed.

"Beasy's? Greenleaf? Amuse? Pasta Piatti?"

"Lots of dinner dates since you've moved to town, Mister Watkins?" She failed to keep the sarcasm out of her voice.

"Lots of *business* dinners, Ms. Payne." He brought her hand up to his mouth and kissed it, his brown eyes now as black with desire as she remembered. "What's your pleasure?"

God damn him. He was playing word games with her. He knew exactly what her pleasure was, and knew he could make her shiver at the mention of it. Which was exactly what she was doing at the moment. Again.

"I'll go change and think about it." She turned to go upstairs. "Make yourself at home while I'm gone. There's wine open in the kitchen. I was about to pour myself a glass when you ca … arrived."

His smile said he knew what the word she almost said was, and he liked it.

Chapter 9

Now what was she going to do? Trace Watkins didn't recognize her from Portland, as she'd feared. No, it was worse, if that was possible. He was Mister Elizabethan Hunk, the man she'd spent the most exciting night of her life with, who'd inhabited her dreams ever since, and who was, it turned out, the manager of the bank she was about to sue. No wonder she'd thought of Halloween when she'd met him and noticed his buff body. And his smile was certainly familiar—that was about all of Romeo's face she'd seen that night.

And here he was, sitting in her living room. Because he wanted to "get to know her?" Really? Or did he want something else?

Like a chance to damage her reputation with what he knew. But if he made public what she'd done, he'd also be telling everyone what he'd done. He'd said so himself. Would he want to start a new job as the town's banker with a rumor of bad behavior?

Maybe, just maybe, he wasn't trying to use Halloween as leverage on her. Should she believe he'd searched for her only because he wanted to see her again? Could she trust he was any different than Paul Dreier in Portland? Didn't what happened on Halloween mean her judgment still wasn't reliable when it came to men?

She looked at the clock. She'd been sitting on her bed running the same thoughts around and around in the squirrel cage of her mind for ten minutes. Time to get changed and see what damage control she needed to do.

She pulled out her favorite dress and boots, hoping they would be armor for the battle, added a little makeup, and spritzed on the perfume she loved. Standing at the top of the stairs, she tried to settle her thoughts before she faced him.

• • •

Trace poured a glass of wine and took it to the living room, where he made himself comfortable, raised the glass in a little toast to his success, and took a sip. He'd done it. He'd found her. His victory lap was short-lived, however. He had to admit, from the tone of her response, finding her might turn out to be the easy part.

Maybe he'd been more impressed with their night together than she'd been.

But that didn't seem right either. Not when she'd reacted to him as she had. When she trembled at his touch, she was no ice queen. And the look in her green eyes tonight sure said she wanted him. But she fought admitting what was only too obvious to them both. Why?

Was there someone else? Not that he'd heard of when he'd asked around town about the ice queen lawyer who was threatening to sue the bank. Nor was there a man around either in October or last night at the brewpub. And if there were another man, wouldn't she have told him right away? It would have been the easiest way to turn him down.

If it wasn't some*one* else, there was some*thing* else. Something he needed to figure out so he could clear it away. Because there was no way in hell he would let her elude him again.

When she returned, she'd changed the jeans and turtleneck sweater she'd been wearing for a short black dress, a denim jacket, a heavy scarf around her neck, and knee-high boots. She was stunning. But then, she could have worn a trash bag, and he'd think the same thing.

He stood as she came into the room. "You look beautiful."

"Thanks." She actually blushed at the compliment.

"Where did you decide you want to eat?"

"Italian, I think. I cleaned all day and didn't take the time to eat much. Pasta always sounds good when I'm hungry."

He waved her to the door and followed. "I can recommend a good cleaning service, if you want to save yourself the work."

"So can I, but I prefer to do it myself. It's a kind of therapy."

"Sounds more like a kind of punishment to me."

"Maybe it's both."

Now what could she need therapy and punishment for? Halloween? Going out to dinner with him? What? She was a mystery he hoped a long dinner with her would solve.

•••

The rain had stopped, and it wasn't too cold. He suggested they walk to the restaurant, and she agreed. As soon as they were settled at their table, the waiter took Trace's order for a bottle of pinot grigio.

When the server left, a silence settled in. Trace hesitated before starting the conversation. It certainly wasn't their first time together, but he thought playing the "first date game" might reassure her he wasn't up to anything bad. What he wanted to do would probably scare the bejesus out of her—he was having one hell of a time keeping his hands to himself. He saw her naked every time he looked at her and would give anything to get her that way again. But his instincts said she needed reassurance, needed to be soothed, not seduced. So, he started with a softball question. "What made you decide to move to Ashland?"

Her eyes narrowed and her mouth pursed for a moment before she answered. He was sure she was weighing each syllable, parsing every sentence he'd spoken, trying to figure out what he was up to and how to react. She must have finally decided the question was innocuous enough to answer. A small smile moved one corner of her mouth incrementally up, and she said, "My transmission."

He was sure he looked as puzzled as he felt. "Explain."

"I was moving back to California when my transmission crapped out on the freeway. I was stuck in Ashland for a week while the shop tracked down what they needed to fix my car." She shrugged her shoulders. "I liked the place and, when I found out there was a law practice on the market, I decided to stay."

"You must have pissed off whoever was holding a job for you in California."

She squirmed uneasily in her chair. "No job waiting. I was just going there."

"You have guts. I'm not sure I could have taken off without a job to go to."

"Not brave at all. I was … never mind. Not important."

The server arrived with their wine, and he and Trace went through the drill of tasting and pouring. When the server left, Trace began, "Now I'm curious. What were you, if not brave?"

She didn't answer but turned the question on him. "Why did you want to leave Portland and come to a small town like Ashland? I assume it had nothing to do with a car part."

He paused, trying to decide whether to pursue the question he'd asked her or stick with his "first date" program. It seemed wiser to let his question go so he laughed before answering hers. "No car parts were injured in my transfer, I promise. I was tired of Portland. Wanted to get back the feeling of community I had in the town where I was raised. So I looked around at possibilities, and there was Ashland. After I was offered the job, I came down for a few days to look around before I accepted. I liked what I found." He took a sip of his wine and hooked her gaze with his. "I very much liked what I found."

She looked down at the table, fiddled with her knife. "Wasn't it a step down from your job in Portland?" When she looked back up, her expression was almost defiant. "Or do you prefer being a big fish in a little pond to being a minnow in the ocean of the city?"

Sure she was making the jab about ponds and fishes to get back at him for his oblique mention of Halloween, he answered only her first question. "Actually, it was a step up. I'm the manager here, probably the youngest in the organization. I was one of a number of officers in Portland. And I'm happier with my life here, which would have made even a step down a good move."

"How do you know you're happy when you've been here less than a month?"

"How did you know Ashland was a good place for you when you'd only been here a week?"

The small smile appeared again. "Point taken. Anyone ever told you you'd make a good attorney?"

"Thanks but I'm not cut out for grad school. I couldn't get away from academia fast enough. I don't like sitting in classrooms. I'd rather learn on the job."

"So, no MBA then."

"Nope. A measly bachelor's degree from the University of New Mexico. You must like academics to have gone on to law school."

"It's probably genetic. My mother has a PhD and teaches Shakespeare. Which is how I ended up as Juliet with sisters named Cordelia and Desdemona. We are unanimous in our dislike of our names but grateful only one of us got stuck as the daughter of King Lear." She looked as if she were challenging him.

"Cordelia isn't bad, even Regan. But Goneril? It would be hell in high school with a name like that. And you were all named for women who died during their plays. Why not Katerina? Or Portia? That would have been a good name for a future lawyer." He cocked his head and lifted his wine glass to her. "Did I pass your test?"

"Sorry. Busted. I should have known. You quoted the balcony scene when we ..." The smile disappeared, she lowered her gaze again, and changed course. "It's a game my sisters and I have played forever to see if people know where our names came from."

He topped off their wine glasses. "I had a modest liberal arts education along with my business courses. Mostly because I was trying to impress a woman. Which apparently is what I'm doing tonight, too."

She squirmed in her seat and moved to yet another subject. "Do you have siblings? And do they have normal names?" she asked.

"I don't know if there's much normal about my twin sister, including her name." He shrugged his shoulders. "Like your parents, mine had strange ideas about what to call their kids. We were christened Tracey and Lacey. I dropped the 'y' at the end of mine because there were two other Traceys in my high school class, and they were both girls. My sister goes by her middle name, Anne, because she hated the whole rhyming name thing."

By this time, Julie was giggling. When she could stop, she asked, "What about your parents?"

"Other than the urge to give their kids cutesy names, nothing too unusual. Father's a banker. Mother was a schoolteacher until she had us and then became a stay-at-home mom. You didn't mention your dad."

She played with the stem of her wine glass, the laughter gone. "My father died when I was in middle school. He was a civil engineer."

Nice going, Watkins. Another detour away from making her comfortable. "I'm sorry. It sounds like you miss him."

"You couldn't have known." She looked up at him with eyes that appeared full. "I do miss him."

The arrival of their salads gave them both a chance to regroup.

An exchange of Ashland gossip accompanied the salad course and then their pasta. By the time coffee arrived, Trace decided she'd calmed down enough for him to try and find out the answer to the question she'd cut off. He had a hunch it might help him understand what was behind her reaction to him.

As he handed her the cream, he asked, "So, to get back to how you came to be in Ashland … if heading to another state without a job and then deciding to change plans in midcourse because you liked the town where your car broke down wasn't brave, what was it?"

•••

Her hand was shaking so hard she could barely hold the pitcher. She should never have made a comment like that. She still hadn't discovered whether he knew about her past in Portland but, even if he didn't, she'd left so many cookie crumbs in their conversation, even the most obtuse person could follow them. Or at least question her about where the crumbs led. And he was far from obtuse.

"I don't really like to talk about what made me decide to move. None of my colleagues or acquaintances in Ashland know. I'd prefer to keep it that way."

He leaned across the table, his dark eyes intense. "Juliet, we are way past the colleagues and acquaintances stage, no matter how brief our relationship has been. You and I know each other in ways most people can only dream about, don't you think?"

Hesitating for a moment while she tried to figure out the safest response, she concluded she couldn't bluff her way past it. He was right. "I guess so. If you mean physically. But what does sex have to do with answering your question?"

"It wasn't just sex."

She looked around quickly to see if anyone was listening.

He didn't seem to notice as he continued. "We made ourselves vulnerable to each other from the first time I smiled at you across your living room. Everything else that happened took what's between us to a whole other level, to someplace amazing, whether you want to admit it or not." He took the pitcher from her still-shaking hand. "Either of us could damage the other if we wanted to. But I would never hurt you. And I don't think you would deliberately hurt me either. Although even if you did, it would still have been worth it."

Leaning back in his chair as if to open up space for her to say what he wanted to hear, he went on. "Nothing you could tell me will change my opinion of you, change the way I feel about you. Nothing will make us any more vulnerable to each other than we already are. Nothing at all."

Why she wanted to tell him, she didn't know. But for the first time since she'd left Portland, the need to have someone know about it, know her side of the story, overwhelmed her. Her eyes closed, she sorted through a half dozen ways to tell him what had happened, trying to find one that put her in a more favorable light. There really wasn't one. So she opened her eyes and started talking.

"Do you remember hearing a while back about a lawyer in Portland who was involved with the Russian mob stealing intellectual property and selling it to the highest bidder?"

"Vaguely."

"He was my boyfriend." She shook her head. "That's not exactly right. I *thought* he was my boyfriend. He was really trying to use me to keep track of what the D.A.'s office was doing."

"You worked for the D.A.?"

"Yeah, I was a deputy D.A. for Multnomah County. And a good one. Until I was investigated by the feds. After that I might as well have been a law clerk. I lost all credibility with my colleagues and the Portland Police Bureau."

"Why? Obviously, you were cleared."

"Yes, of course I was. I hadn't told him anything. He told the FBI I hadn't. So did I. So did all my friends who were interviewed. Legally, I was off the hook. But not in the minds of everyone around me." She poured herself the last of the wine and downed it in one gulp. "My bad judgment in being involved with him was a 'career-limiting move,' to quote my former boss. When I couldn't take any more of the snubs and cold shoulders, the assignments a paralegal could handle blindfolded, I quit."

"Why would they blame you? No one else knew he was a crook, did they?"

"Everyone in the legal community knew he skated very close to the edge of the law, maybe over. But in my arrogance, I thought I knew better than the rest of my peers. After all, the guy had the good taste to want me. I didn't read the other signs—his curiosity about my job, the questions about what I was working on. I thought he was interested in my life, and dismissed his other questions with something noncommittal. I was so sure no man would ever use me, convinced he was after me for my brains and looks, not my job. I didn't put two and two together until it was too late."

Trace's sinful smile appeared again. "You were right about one thing—any man who's introduced to you would be attracted to your brains and your looks."

"Don't. It's not funny."

"I'm not being funny. I'm telling the truth." This time when he leaned over the table he took her hands in his. "Jesus, Juliet, there's not a person alive who hasn't made a bad call with a relationship. Why are you so hard on yourself?"

"Because I didn't think it was possible for me to make a bad call about a man, about anything, really. I didn't think I had ever made a misstep, even a little one, much less a judgment call bad enough to trigger a federal investigation."

From the expression on his face, he was trying hard not to break out in a grin—or a laugh. "You have me there. I've never heard of anyone who did that. But, beautiful, can't you cut yourself some slack? Even if you made one mistake, what makes you think you'll repeat it?"

"I already did. On Halloween. I'd never done anything so outrageous, so risky. Not even Greer at her worst would have." She withdrew her hands from his.

"You think I go around doing things like that? No one who knows me would believe it if I told them what happened. I'm the most dedicated rule-follower you'll ever meet. Halloween was something unique, something special. And who's Greer?"

"Greer was the name I went by for most of my adult life; that's who I was in Portland. When I moved to Ashland I changed my name back to what people called me when I was growing up—Julie, for Juliet, as you figured out. I'd been Greer since high school because I hated the teasing about being Juliet."

"So … the problem is, you're worried people will think our behavior on Halloween won't reflect well on the person you want to be here. Right? With your reputation in town, I doubt there's anything you could do short of terrorism to change people's opinions of you."

Frowning at the idea of people talking about her, she asked, "How do you know what people think? You're new in town. No one would tell you anything."

"Unless the new banker in town is asking about the lawyer who's threatening to sue him."

"You asked people about me?" The frown was much deeper now.

"Of course I did. Didn't you ask around about me?

"That's different."

"No, it's not. And what happened between us on Halloween …"

"'What happened between us' sounds like we were holding hands and exchanging phone numbers. It sure doesn't sound like hooking up with a perfect stranger and spending hours in his motel room without even knowing what he really looked like or what his name was."

"When you describe it that way, it does sound a bit …"

"Sleazy?"

"I was going for impulsive." He tented his fingers and rested his chin on them. "I'd never have suspected the woman who barged into my office and terrified me the first day of my new job would be so insecure about herself."

She tried hard not to look smug. "I terrified you? Really?"

"Well, maybe not terrified, but certainly intimidated. You're missing the point of my comment. Are you really so insecure about the way people view you here?"

"No, not when I make good decisions about … stuff."

"Meaning men?"

"Okay, yes, men."

Reaching across the table, he took her hand again and wouldn't let it go. "And how many men have you made decisions about since you moved to Ashland, Ms. Payne?"

"One, and look where it got me."

"It got *me* an amazing night with a beautiful woman and dinner with her tonight. I hope, after all the time I've spent trying to find her again, it won't be the end of what it gets me."

"I don't understand. Did you think if you found me you'd have an advantage you could use?"

"Juliet, I'm not the guy in Portland. I'm not trying to use you. Jesus, I've done everything except walk through town in the damn costume to see if you'd recognize me. Don't I get some points for effort? I even tried to track down the kind of perfume you wear."

"My perfume? Why?"

"I thought it would give me a clue to who you were, to help find you. I know it makes no sense, but I was desperate. Anyway, the two times I've seen you before tonight, you didn't smell like you did on Halloween so it wouldn't have helped."

"I don't wear this perfume during the day. It's too heavy."

"Put me out of this particular misery, will you? What's it called?"

She shook her head, sighed, and looked at him. "Passion."

"Ah, so it does."

"Does what?"

"Give me a clue as to who you really are."

Chapter 10

The walk back to her house was a little wetter and much quieter than the walk to the restaurant had been. When they reached the door, Julie rummaged in her purse for her keys, playing for time, trying to figure out what she wanted to say next.

Trace was standing close enough that she swore she could feel the heat of his body. She could certainly smell his cologne. She wasn't sure she was ready to let either sensation go. But the evening was over. Wasn't it? Shouldn't it be?

She put the key in the lock.

There. That decided it. Evening over. I'm going into my house. Alone.

"Well, I guess this is goodnight. Thank you for dinner. I enjoyed it. I'd invite you in but ..." She struggled to articulate a reason that made any sense.

Trace rescued her. "It's okay. I've had a great evening, and I don't want to push my luck."

"Thank you again."

"For dinner? You already thanked me."

"No, not for dinner. For not making me feel stupid or paranoid because I was sure you were up to something underhanded."

"For the record, I try not to be underhanded in any aspect of my life, but you're welcome." He paused for two heartbeats, then added, "Anything else you want to thank me for?"

She saw the look in his eyes and knew it would only take a bit of encouragement for him to kiss her. "Probably, but that's all I'm willing to admit to at the moment."

He put his hands on her shoulders. "Not exactly what I was hoping for, but I'll take it." He leaned in and kissed her forehead. "I'm glad I found you, Juliet. But I want *you* to be glad, too. I don't want you to feel hunted and trapped. So, the next move is yours. If you want to, call me next week, and we can do something together. Or just talk. Whatever. It's up to you."

"Okay. Thank you. Again." His hands were still on her shoulders. The memory of what those hands had felt like in other places came rushing back, making her shiver. She wanted them someplace else, any place, every place on her body.

The long conversation in the restaurant, which she'd hoped would make it possible to walk away—or force him to walk away—had, instead, made her want him even more. He'd been open, sincere, and hot as hell. If he didn't leave soon, she'd make the next move, all right. She'd move so she could feel her body against his. She'd kiss his delicious mouth, feel his arms lock around her, taste the parts of him she'd missed in the motel room.

Door. Unlock door. Get inside. Before I do something impulsive. Again.

"Good night, Juliet. Sweet dreams." He dropped another kiss on her forehead and went down the steps from her porch. She was almost safe on the other side of the door, when he turned back. "Wait. I haven't given you my cell number. So you can call if you want."

"I have your number at the bank."

"Might be better to separate the personal and professional."

"You're right. Not such a good idea to call while we're both working. Come on in while I get a piece of paper and something to write with."

He took the steps to the porch two at a time as if afraid she might change her mind if he took too long.

And then he was in her space again. She wanted him to go before she could think any more about what had happened to shift the atmosphere between them from dark to light. From stop to go. So she could relegate to the back of her mind the niggling thought maybe Halloween hadn't been a meaningless hookup after all. A little piece of information presently scaring her more than she was willing to admit.

When she gave him a pad of sticky notes and a pen, their fingers brushed. She saw his eyes darken, felt her breath stop and the blood leave her brain from the most minor of touches. She was getting in deeper by the second.

He wrote his number down, tore off the paper, took her hand, and slowly turned it palm up. After he placed the sticky note and the pen in her hand, he closed her fingers over them. "I don't want you to lose this," he said, his voice low and tight. "It's important to me, very important, you use it." He didn't let go of her, and she didn't pull her hand away. Nor did she break eye contact with him.

The urgency in his voice. The sincerity in his eyes. The heat from his hand. It was happening all over again. How could he do this to her when he had barely touched her?

"I better go," he said, releasing her hand.

He had the door open, when she thought again of the only question she wanted him to answer. "Trace, what's the *real* reason you tried so hard to find me?"

His hand still on the doorknob he said, "It's what I said before. When I woke up the morning after Halloween and you were gone, the only thing I could think of was finding you. I didn't want the night to be just some fantasy. I wanted it to be real. Wanted to make it real. And I needed to know if you felt the same."

His words took her breath away. She believed him, absolutely and completely. Her last defense was gone. He'd been across the moat in the restaurant when he'd said he was vulnerable to her. Now he was inside the wall. And she knew it was where she wanted him to be.

"Maybe you shouldn't go," she whispered.

When he faced her, he looked bewildered. She almost laughed. She had spent the evening up until now pushing him away because she was confused. Now she was pulling him toward her, and it was his turn to be puzzled.

"What're you saying?" he asked.

"You said I should make the next move. I'm making it. I want you to stay." She dropped the pen and pad of sticky notes, took the few steps she needed to reach him, and slid her arms under his jacket and around his waist. "Please, Trace?"

He slammed the door shut. Tugging at her to get her closer, he fit her body to his. With one hand he tipped up her face. "Are you sure, Juliet? We're not playing fantasy this time."

"Yes, I'm sure. This time it's the real us." On tiptoes, clutching the front of his shirt to bring him closer to her, she pressed her lips to his mouth. The initial contact was soft, but within seconds the kiss was wild, hot, almost frantic, as if they were picking up where they'd left off on Halloween. She could feel his arousal against her belly, felt her insides melting into a liquid heat, thrilling and exciting her.

Then he took control of them both, slowing them down, as if he wanted to savor her, make this sweet, hot contact between them last. His tongue tasted her top lip; his teeth nipped at her lower lip. She shivered at the pleasure of having his mouth on hers, of once again tasting the sheer maleness of him, feeling the sensuous slide of his tongue over hers.

When he broke away from the kiss, she made a soft sound of disappointment and tried to pull him back to her, but he resisted.

"Maybe … I don't know … maybe this isn't such a good idea. Tonight, I mean. Not that I don't want to, but maybe we shouldn't." His whispered objections rang false to her.

"Why?" she asked. "We've already been down this road, and it led, you said, to the best night of your life."

"I want you; you know that. But I don't want you to have reservations or regrets. I don't want to play hide and seek with you again if you get cold feet tomorrow or next week. And if I kiss you again, I won't remember that, won't care that it matters. So maybe I better leave until you have time to think this evening over."

"I don't need to think it over any more. You've answered every question I had. Said I was the one who'd decide what's next. Didn't you mean what you said?"

He kissed the tip of her nose, amusement in his eyes. "Yes, beautiful, I meant it. You get to decide."

"Then stay. It's what I want. Without reservations, without regrets, and no more hide and seek."

"Jesus, Juliet, I thought you'd run out of ways to astonish me. I've never met anyone like you before." His voice was husky, intense.

No one had ever looked at her the way Trace was looking at her now. As if she were the only woman on the planet, the only woman worth dying for, the only woman worth living for, the only woman who could satisfy him.

"Is that good?" she asked.

"Let me show you how good it is."

He pulled her tight against him one more time, and his mouth came down hard on hers, demanding, taking what he wanted, the way she remembered him from Halloween. Responding to him, she raked her fingers through his hair, tangled her tongue with his, bit his lip. All the air was gone from her lungs, and she was sure she'd fall if he didn't keep her upright.

It was like the first kiss in his motel room. Only better. This time she knew who he was, and she liked it even more. When the kiss ended, she sighed. "I thought I'd imagined how good this was."

"Kissing?"

"Kissing you, holding you, the smell of you, the way you taste. It's all as good as I remembered. Maybe better."

"Let's go see if we can jog your memory about anything else."

"Masks and no lights this time, too?"

"I haven't decided yet."

She'd never known a smirk could be sexy, but his definitely was. "You like being bossy in bed, don't you?"

"We're not in bed, but no, I don't usually. Something about you brings it out in me. Does it bother you?"

"Actually, it kinda turns me on."

"Good to know. Next time, I'll bring the whips and chains."

"That bossy definitely does *not* turn me on. And what makes you think there'll be a next time?"

"Oh, there'll be a next time, Juliet. But I got the message. Masks—yes. Whips and chains—no. How do you feel about handcuffs and rope?"

"Are we going to talk about going to bed, or are we going there?"

"We are definitely going to bed, beautiful, as soon as you lead me to it."

Chapter 11

Not wanting to startle her into changing her mind, Trace forced himself to take his time, to remove his jacket and carefully place it on the back of a chair, then walk, not run, up the steps behind Julie. He hadn't been sure she'd even see him, let alone make love with him again. And then in one short, heartfelt speech, he'd apparently found the words to convince her he was for real. And now what he'd thought earlier in the evening might never happen again was about to.

As soon as they got to her room, she began to shed her scarf. He stopped her hands. "Let me. I want to take all the wrapping off in the light so I can see every inch of you."

"So you've decided about the lights, have you?" Although he felt her shiver at his touch, she sounded as if she was trying to maintain the same easy tone of conversation from downstairs.

He went along with her. "Yup. You said you had poor night vision. I want to be considerate."

She laughed, but it sounded tight and nervous. "Oh, you remember that, do you? What else do you remember?"

He slid her jacket off her shoulders and dropped it on the floor. "Let's see." He unzipped her dress, leaned in, and kissed a spot behind her ear. "You like being kissed there." He'd slipped her dress off and softly caressed from her neck and shoulders around to her back. "I remember your skin feels like silk." He unhooked her bra and removed it. "And you like this." He ducked his head and sucked at her nipple.

"Oh, God, you remember all the right things," she said, her voice now thick and sultry.

He sat her on the edge of her bed and found the zippers on her boots. When they came off, she was left dressed in only her thong, much like the last time they were together.

He ripped at the buttons on the front of his shirt and yanked the shirttail out from his trousers. Taking it slow was now lost in his need to get naked and close to her. His shoes and socks were off, and he was about to unfasten his belt when she reached for the buckle. Looking down, all he could see was the glow of desire in her green eyes.

"Let me," she whispered. The belt was open, then his fly unzipped and his trousers were gone, along with his boxers. "This is what I remember," she said as she circled his penis with her fingers and began to rub, gently at first but more firmly as he got harder and larger from her touch.

Her eyes held his as she worked on him until suddenly, it was not only her hand on him, but also her mouth. Groaning, he pushed forward into her. She was rubbing, then sucking and licking, cupping his balls. It was like the most erotic of his dreams about her, and he never wanted her to stop, but if she didn't, he'd come in her mouth. Not what he wanted. Not what he thought she wanted, either.

"Juliet, please, you need to stop."

She looked up at him with a wicked smile. "Oh, did I remember wrong and you don't like it?"

"I like it too much." He took her hands and pushed her back onto the bed.

She sat up and brushed away his hands. "Wait. Condoms."

He laughed as he snagged his trousers from the floor and rummaged around in the pocket.

"Do you always have protection handy?" she asked. "And why do you laugh when I ask? You did the last time, too."

"I was laughing at myself for being a good Boy Scout this time, I guess. I don't usually carry condoms around with me. It was wishful thinking tonight. On Halloween, it was because a college buddy thought it was funny to provide us with protection in case we scored with the women at your party."

"And you did—with me." She closed her eyes, and he could feel the slight stiffness in her body that said she wasn't with him anymore.

He took her chin in his hand, and said, "Look at me, please." When she did he said, "It was no hookup. I am not using you. You are not Greer. You're Juliet. And you're mine." He kissed her with as much passion and intensity as he was capable of, trying to reinforce his words.

•••

How could someone who seemed on the surface to be so conventional be so good with romantic words? Everything he'd said all evening had touched her in some deeply emotional way. He knew her secrets, yet said he wanted to see if they could take this connection between them further. He clearly wanted her, yet he let her make the decision to be together. And he said she was his.

Now he was commanding her with his eyes to look deep and see there what she had heard him say. What she saw left her breathless. She couldn't look away from the heat of his gaze, the desire she'd never seen so strong in any man's eyes. It burned through any objections she might have. If she had any left.

"Let me love you, Juliet." Tucking the condom under the pillow on his side of the bed, he slid in beside her. "Tell me what you need. What you want."

"You. I want you. Any way I can have you. Every way I can have you. I've wanted you since the first time I saw you in my living room. It hasn't changed."

"You're very good at pretending otherwise."

This time she kissed him. "Shh. Don't remind me."

"How 'bout I remind you of other things?" He skimmed his hand along her body, from her hip up, lightly touching, raising goose bumps along her side. When he reached her breast, he dropped his head. He cupped her breast and added the feel of his mouth on her nipple to the sensations his hand had produced. His tongue brought the nipple to a diamond-hard point, then his teeth gently scraped over it.

"Oh, yes," she whispered. "I like that."

His mouth closed over the other nipple, his tongue licking and his mouth sucking. Words weren't possible anymore, only moans of pleasure.

Her hands roamed over his body, felt the muscles in his shoulders, in his back, flex and contract as he explored her. He'd pulled back enough to allow her access to the hard surface of his chest, softened with a cloud of hair as black as his eyes. Combing her fingers through the hair, she moved up his neck to feel the stubble of his beard and to nibble on his lips again.

So busy with her own explorations, she didn't realize he had moved one hand to the delta of curls guarding her sex until she felt him cup her there. Her sharp intake of breath made him stop and ask, "Juliet?"

She lay back, her eyes half closed, and exhaled. Then said merely, "Oh, yes."

It was all the permission he seemed to need. Gently he separated the folds of her sex, found the nub of her clitoris, and began to caress it with the heel of his hand, slowly at first but as her breathing accelerated, so did the speed of his hand. She rocked her hips, rubbing herself against his hand, reaching for release, her hands gripping the sheets. Then his fingers entered her, found the perfect place inside her, and with one touch, she saw stars. Stars, moons, fireworks, and heaven.

When she came back to earth, he was nuzzling her neck, stroking her breast, insinuating his knee between her legs, beginning to build the need in her again. But she wanted something else first. Catching him off balance as he shifted his weight, she managed to turn him on his back and straddle him, pressing her sex against his erection, pinning his hands to the pillow beneath his head.

She knew he could reverse her move with little or no effort, but his grin said he wasn't going to.

"Now what, beautiful?"

"Now I get to enjoy tasting your gorgeous body." Matching her actions to her words, she pressed her breasts against his chest while she nibbled her way around his jawline to one ear, where she licked and blew softly, murmuring as she did, "You taste so good. Every part of you."

It was his turn to squirm. She could feel his hips under hers moving, pressing, grinding against her. She thought he must be on the brink of exploding. His desire stoked her own as gradually she, too, began to rock her pelvis.

"Condom, Juliet. Now," he said through gritted teeth.

She groped beneath the pillow, but, paying more attention to the press of his erection against her than to her quest, she couldn't find what she was looking for. Taking advantage of her distraction, he flipped her onto her back, found the foil packet, ripped it open with his teeth, and handed it to her.

"Hurry, get this on me."

Hands shaky with need, she complied. When he was covered, he entered her with one swift thrust. But after a few strokes he stilled.

"I love how you feel when you're inside me," she whispered. "You don't know how good it feels."

He pulled his head back far enough so she could see his smile. "I have a fairly good idea how it feels, don't you think?"

She laughed. Not only was sex with this man earth shattering, but it was also fun. "Yes, I guess you do."

"As good as you remember?"

"Better. I can see your face this time."

Then he began to move again, pulling out of her almost all the way, then driving back in. Slowly at first. Then harder. Faster. Taking her with him as they swirled around and around, climbing, looking for relief from the need growing with each stroke. Finding the world in each other's arms.

As her orgasm overtook her, she cried out, "Trace, oh, my God, Trace!" and with one last thrust, he came, too.

Chapter 12

Trace held her, kissing the top of her head, stroking her arm, murmuring unintelligible sounds because he wasn't capable of putting a sentence together. She had once again blown the top of his head off with her passion, her total immersion in their lovemaking. He was riding a swift current over a steep hill, falling faster and faster into a bottomless whirlpool with this woman. And he didn't care.

Julie stirred in his arms. "Thank you."

"What for this time?" He kissed her softly.

"For finding me."

"There was never any question I would, Juliet, if it had taken me until I was cashing in my IRA." Hugging her closer, he continued, "I wanted to hear what I heard tonight too badly."

"What did you hear tonight?" she asked.

"You said my name when you came."

"What did I say before?"

"It was something like, 'oh, God, oh, God, oh, God.'"

"Ah, the orgasm prayer."

He snorted. "Where the hell did you hear that?"

"Just made it up. Why?"

"I'm not sure I'll ever be able to hear some clergyman say 'oh, God,' again without thinking of you and orgasms."

"Nice to know I've left my mark on you."

He tilted her face so he could look at her straight on. "You have no idea what a mark you've left on me."

"Enough so you'll stay the night?"

"Will I have to sneak out the back tomorrow morning?"

"We'll worry about tomorrow when it gets here." She yawned and stretched. It was such a sensuous move, he was tempted to try for one more round of sex. But she looked tired and emotionally drained. Now that he'd found her, had loved her again, there would be time for more later.

Turning her so her back was against his chest, he whispered, "Time to sleep, beautiful." He put his arm around her waist and his foot over hers, and felt her relax against him. In minutes, her breathing was even, and her body completely lax. She was asleep.

He fought joining her. Wrapped around her, absorbing the soft feel of her skin, the sound of her breath, the scent of her perfume mingled with the smell of sex and his soap, he didn't think he'd ever been so content.

• • •

Julie woke at first light after the best night's sleep she'd had in forever. Apparently Trace was not only a good dinner companion and an amazing lover, but he was also an effective sleeping aid. He was still draped around her; she didn't think either of them had moved all night.

"Good morning." The greeting came from behind her, accompanied by a kiss on the shoulder.

"It is a good morning, isn't it?" She wriggled out of his arms and rolled over.

He touched her face. "Indeed it is. I've spent a lot of mornings over the past month or so being pissed off because I dreamed about a mysterious woman in a mask and then woke up to find out she wasn't there. It is one hell of a lot better to wake up and find her beside me."

"Then let's celebrate. How about breakfast at Brothers' with the morning paper?"

"I haven't been to Brothers' since Fred and I ate there the morning after your party. Let's do it." He started to slide out from under the covers.

"Oh, hell. That's it."

"What's it?" He turned back toward her with a puzzled look on his face.

"That first meeting, in your office. Part of the reason I thought you recognized me was I thought you looked familiar to me, too, but I couldn't place you. Now I can." She fought hard to keep a grin from breaking out. "What do you remember about that breakfast at Brothers' with your friend?"

"Let's see … the eggs were perfectly done. The bacon was a little too crisp. The toast was good."

"That's it? That's all you remember?"

"Well, I remember having two lattes dumped in my lap, but I don't imagine that's what you mean."

"Actually, it *is* what I mean."

"How did you know …?"

"I'm sorta … kinda … maybe I'm the person who put those lattes there."

He stared at her for a second or two, then burst out laughing. When he stopped, he took her face in his hand and said, "I looked at every face in the whole damn place, every dark-haired woman on the street, looking for the one woman I wanted to find. Turns out, she tried to get my attention, and I didn't notice."

"Don't ascribe a good motive to me. I was so busy looking around to make sure no one was there who might know what I'd done the night before, I didn't see I was on a collision course with the waiter."

He skated his hand along her waist and hip. "The real Romeo and Juliet didn't have this much trouble recognizing each other, did they?"

"The real Romeo and Juliet, assuming you mean the Shakespeare characters, died at the end of the play." She picked up his hand and kissed each knuckle. "Let's not get too carried away with that particular metaphor."

"Good point." He returned the kisses on her hand. "Let's go get breakfast."

"And then do something fun."

"The kind of fun that we have naked?"

"I was thinking more of the kind with clothes on. Outdoors. It's supposed to be clear today. Maybe for the last time this month, who knows? We should take advantage of it. Are you an outdoor person?"

"Yeah."

"Where's your favorite place to hike?"

"I haven't been here long enough to find it."

"Lucky for you, I happen to know a bunch of places."

"Okay, but first fun things first," he said as he pressed his erection against her.

• • •

After breakfast, they hiked up the Pilot Rock trail so she could show him the stunning views of Southern Oregon and Northern California at the trail's end. Dinner back at Julie's house capped off their weekend.

After they'd eaten, Julie brought up something she'd been mulling over all day.

"I think you should know, I'm going to recuse myself from the negotiations with the bank. I'll find another lawyer for my clients and get myself off the hook I'm on at the moment."

"What hook? When you thought I wanted you to back off, you said you'd never desert your clients. Why now?"

"That was when I thought you might try to … well, to … persuade me, shall we say, by revealing my Portland past."

"Why is it different because you're sleeping with me?"

"Because it is. Don't you see? They at least need to know we're seeing each other socially. If I don't tell them and they find out, which they will, it'll look like I'm trying to hide something."

"Suppose it doesn't matter to them."

"Then I'll stay with them. And if it does matter, I'll leave. It's that simple."

"If it's any help, the news I called to give you on Friday was the bank is prepared to make whole everyone who had money stolen from their accounts. It will also help them with credit watches on their credit scores for as long as needed."

"Really? You found the weakness in your security program?"

"The head of IT still doesn't understand what happened. He can't find anything wrong with the security program; there's no evidence of hacking. He and his crew are still working on it. But the bank wants to make a good faith effort to keep our customers happy, even if we haven't figured out what happened yet."

"Can I pass this along to my clients—my ex-clients—whichever they turn out to be?"

"Absolutely. When you meet with them, give them my news, then tell them our news. See what they say. I'm betting they won't be turning down the best damn lawyer in the county because she's sleeping with the bank manager."

"Oh, for God's sake, I'm not telling them we're sleeping together."

"Are you distracting me with the orgasm prayer on purpose?" He drew her hand to his mouth and kissed it.

"That's not the orgasm prayer, and you know it. You're trying to change the subject."

"Yeah, I am. I was hoping a mention of orgasm would remind you how good it feels to have one. Then I can get you back in bed one more time before I leave and go home to my lonely but considerably larger bed which, by the way, would be much more comfortable for the two of us."

"I know. I deliberately bought a double bed instead of a queen or king to remind myself I was going to live a more discrete life."

"Why not a single, then?"

"Too nun-like."

"I had no idea bed sizes represented points on a moral compass that judged one's life choices. I thought it was about having a comfortable place to sleep."

"Well, now you know. It isn't that simple."

Chapter 13

Julie moved the furniture around in her tiny conference room, and changed the way the cookies were arranged on the plate and the napkins were displayed, trying to keep busy waiting for the arrival of her client group's leaders. She'd already practiced the speech she planned to give more times than she'd practiced some of her opening and closing statements to juries. Neither the speech prep nor the cookie rearranging was working to calm her down, however.

It was a relief when the first arrivals made an appearance. As usual, Martha Combes, a longtime local activist who'd become a friend in addition to a client, was early. She was followed shortly after by two men Julie had met when she'd given a talk at the senior center. The remaining representatives, two students from the university, were late, as they often were because of class schedules. Julie tried for small talk while they waited, but chitchat was harder for her than usual. She hoped no one noticed. Eventually the two students arrived, and after the preliminaries were out of the way, Julie launched into her speech.

"First, I want to tell you about the progress we've made with the bank in getting things under control. The head of their IT department has been personally looking into this, and he can't find any security breeches or evidence of hacking."

One of the older men snorted. "Then he has no business running an IT department."

The other one said, "Maybe the Chinese military or some bored kid in a basement in Ukraine is smarter than he is."

Julie continued as if she hadn't heard. "However, as a gesture of goodwill to their customers, while they continue to investigate, they've offered to cover the losses of anyone who had money taken from their accounts. They'll also get surveillance put on everyone's credit records for a year or longer if problems arise."

"That's it? That's what we're gonna get for all this trouble?" one student said.

"It's their opening offer, a good-faith gesture. But remember I said this wouldn't be the big casino payout you were hoping for," Julie said. She'd tried several times to explain to this guy that getting a huge settlement from the bank was unlikely, unless they could prove significant damages. He hadn't listened then. He wasn't listening now.

"And before you hear it from someone who saw us, you should know I … ah … I went to dinner with Trace Watkins, the new bank manager, over the weekend. And he's asked me to have dinner with him again this week." She was sure she was blushing. But her omission of sex on the list of things she was doing with Trace didn't seem to fool Martha, who had what could only be described as a leer on her face. "I had no intention of seeing him socially but … well, it happened when he contacted me on Saturday about the offer from the bank. We got to talking and …" She let the sentence trail off.

She tried to read the faces of those sitting around the table, but other than Martha's, she couldn't. "No suit has been filed yet, and I'm still hopeful we can come to agreement on a settlement. But I completely understand if you think I have a conflict of interest now and you want me to remove myself from the negotiations."

"Remove yourself?" Martha said. "Hell no. Honey, you are now sitting in the catbird seat. Mister Tall, Dark, and Yummy isn't stupid. He'll do whatever it takes to impress you. Up to and including making sure you get a good settlement for your clients."

"Yeah," the disgruntled student said, "or she'll do whatever it takes to keep him interested and sabotage the case."

"This is where I leave so you can discuss those different ways of looking at it," Julie said. "I'll abide by your decision. If you want another attorney, I'll help you look and will, of course, make sure there's a smooth transition." She rose to leave. "You know where the coffee and cookies are. I'll go back to my office while you talk. Someone come get me when you've made a decision."

Surprisingly, it took them less than ten minutes to make a decision and send Martha to deliver the news.

"We don't want you to back out, Julie. You were willing to take this case on when no one else would, and you've been upfront with us all along about everything. We don't see why this will change things." She had a twinkle in her brown eyes. "And on a personal note, honey? I'm happy it's you who snagged him. If I were forty years younger, I'd give you a run for your money, but since I'm not, I'm glad it's you."

Julie could hardly wait to tell Trace he had an admirer.

• • •

The remainder of the year went by quickly. Trace became a welcome and influential presence in the business community. Julie's practice continued to be interesting. They spent time together every weekend, enjoying each other's company as well as what Ashland's restaurants and theaters had to offer. Julie got to know Fred Arnett and Amber Lake, who'd returned from her TV stint tanned and fit but not the big winner. They told Fred and Amber a version of how, on Halloween night, Trace had seen Julie on the street and he'd looked for her ever since he'd been back in Ashland, only recognizing her when he saw her tattoo. They didn't include the details of what had followed on Halloween, although Julie thought Fred had his suspicions, and Amber looked about to ask Trace a question or two before the subject got changed.

Just before New Year's, Trace held the open house he'd been planning, with Julie acting as official hostess. They referred to it between themselves as their "coming out" party. Not that the whole town didn't already know about their relationship. After their fourth or fifth appearance together in a restaurant, a movie theater, or at a play, it was common knowledge. He heard it from his employees at work. She heard it from her theater friends and her book club.

The bank fraud mystery was still unsolved, although everyone who'd lost money had been made whole, and no more withdrawals from bank accounts had occurred. It seemed like everything was returning to normal.

Then the Oregon Shakespeare Festival opened a new season.

Since the opening coincided with Julie's birthday, Trace planned a celebration with dinner at Pasta Piatti, where they'd had their first dinner together, and tickets to the Festival's opening production of *Twelfth Night*. It was a perfect romantic evening. Julie even thought he might finally tell her he loved her.

But her past intervened.

As they were waiting in the Bowmer Theater's lobby for the doors to open so they could take their seats, Julie heard a familiar voice call a now not-so-familiar name.

"Greer? Greer Payne? Is that you? It is, isn't it?"

She closed her eyes and thought about ignoring the voice. However, when Trace gave her a questioning look complete with raised eyebrow, she knew he'd heard it, too. Reluctantly she turned to face the owner of the voice. "Hi, Margo. Yeah, it's me."

Margo Keyes, a deputy D.A. in Portland and one of the only people who had supported her in the aftermath of the scandal, was standing five feet away. Margo's husband, his Portland Police Bureau colleague, and the colleague's wife, were twenty feet away. All four of them were staring at Julie with surprised looks on their faces.

Her former associate hugged her. "It's good to see you," Margo said. "Did you come up from California for the plays?"

"Not exactly. I live in Ashland." Before Margo could react, Julie said, "Margo, this is Trace Watkins. Trace, Margo Keyes."

The two acknowledged the introduction, but Margo immediately returned to the first statement. "You live here? I thought you moved to California. No wonder no one has been able to find you."

"Long story." Julie didn't feel like going into how she'd landed here in her new hometown, and she wasn't going to bite on the last sentence either. Anyone from Portland looking for her would most likely be trying to find a way to further humiliate her.

"You're not with the Jackson County D.A.'s office, are you? No, I guess I can answer my own question. We'd have known if you were."

"I'm in private practice."

When the announcement came that the doors were open for the audience to move into the theater, Julie said, "Looks like it's time to take our seats. You'd better get back to your husband. Enjoy the play."

Margo seemed to want to continue the conversation but didn't argue. "Maybe we could have a drink afterwards? Catch up? There's something I think you should know ..."

"Sorry. We have plans."

"Oh, well, then ... Anyway, it was good to see you." Margo hugged her again. Julie didn't hug back.

When Margo had gone back to her husband and friends, Trace said, "Brrr. It's gonna take me a few minutes to defrost here. The ice queen is back." He shivered and brushed off his arms, as if to remove snow.

"Was I so bad?"

"Beautiful, you could have frozen Ashland Creek solid."

"I didn't mean to be rude."

"Yes, you did. Who is she anyway?"

Julie explained.

"I've never heard you mention her before. Not a close friend then?"

"Not close, no. But she was a friend, I guess. Really more of a colleague."

"Obviously, you haven't been in touch since you left Portland, or she would have known you were here. She caught you off balance. Is that why you were so cool?"

"Or maybe it was being called Greer. It's been a long time."

"Do you think it might have been a good idea to agree to a drink? For old times' sake?"

"I don't know what we have to catch up on, and I really don't think I care to have them know what I'm doing now."

She hoped the expression on her face told him the subject was closed.

In spite of being seated on the opposite side of the theater from the Portlanders, to Julie, the foursome seemed to be in a spotlight with an imaginary neon arrow flashing "here be dragons." Or something. She was aware of every move one of them made, every glance over at her, every laugh, every rustle of a program. Luckily the lights went down, the first act began, and she lost herself in the play.

Then came the intermission.

Excusing herself, she went downstairs and got in the long line outside the ladies' room. As she shuffled ahead, foot by foot, she wondered how she was going to avoid Margo and her cohort at the end of the play. Maybe she and Trace could go out the handicap access door, which opened onto the brick courtyard shared by the two major theaters. Then all they'd have to do would be …

"Greer, good. I have a chance to talk to you." She turned to the woman behind Julie. "Mind if I stand in line with my friend? I don't want to use the ladies' room, just talk with her."

It was Margo, and Julie did mind. But she couldn't bring herself to say so. Neither did the woman behind Julie.

"I don't use my middle name anymore, Margo. I'm Julie here."

"Julie, huh? You don't seem like a Julie to me. But then, I always knew you as Greer. Anyway, Gr … ah, Julie … I'm glad to see you again. You look happy. And I can understand part of it by looking at the guy you're with. Who is he?"

"He's the manager of the Northwest Savings and Loan here."

"Is it serious? It looks like it is."

"I guess." Julie lifted her chin and snapped out, "Why this interest in someone I'm with, Margo? You've never cared this much before. What exactly is it you're dancing around?"

Margo's eyes shifted to the side, and her slight shoulder shrug said how embarrassed she was to be caught. "I shouldn't have tried to be sneaky. You always were good at reading a witness."

If I'd been that good, I'd have figured out Paul Dreier, wouldn't I? You're up to something, and you think flattering me will get it.

As if reading her thoughts, Margo said, "You're right. There *is* something I want to talk about with you. It's about the office."

"Don't waste your breath or my time. I don't want to talk about it now or ever."

"Please, let me explain." Margo lowered her voice. "I don't want to embarrass or upset you, but I think you should know you're missed."

Julie snorted in disbelief. "Yeah, right. Like a case of shingles would be missed."

"I'm serious. No one in the office has your knowledge and ability with fraud cases. Because of that, we've had a hard time with a couple prosecutions recently. It's clear we need someone with your skill set. Jeff's been looking for you. He wants to talk to you."

More flattery? Maybe not. It was true the fraud cases had always been hers to prosecute because she'd done it well. Even now, it was still what she liked doing. And the D.A. was trying to find her? To talk about what?

Margo answered both questions before Julie could ask them. "There's an opening in the office, and for a change, we have enough money in the budget to fill it. Jeff's been trying to track you down to see if you'd be interested. Well, I guess more accurately, to see if he could persuade you to be interested."

"In going back to Portland?" She couldn't hide the shock she felt at Margo's suggestion.

"I understand you probably don't have a lot of fond memories of the office. But what happened two years ago is water under the bridge, over the dam, wherever water goes in clichés. What happened is old news. People appreciate what you brought to the party. Would you give it some thought?"

"I doubt it. But thanks." Julie was at the head of the line and relieved the uncomfortable conversation would soon be over.

"At least can I tell Jeff where you are so he can contact you himself and talk to you?"

"I can't keep him from finding me now that you know where I am." Julie scuttled into the empty stall without saying goodbye and locked the door. She wasn't sure if she wanted to laugh or cry. They wanted her back. At least so Margo said. It was hard to believe, after what had happened and how she'd been treated.

After she finished in the ladies room, Julie took some time to compose herself before she returned to her seat. The conversation with Margo must have still shown, however, because Trace said, "You were gone a long time. And you look stressed. Something happen?"

She almost told him, but brushed it off, "Long line, as usual." She'd think about it and tell him after the play.

• • •

"You're quiet. Not too impressed with the production? I thought they did a great job," Trace said as they walked back to her house after the play.

"No, I liked it fine. It's just …" She wasn't sure how he was going to react to this, so she wanted to be careful how she told him about the conversation with Margo. "When I was in line for the ladies' room, Margo joined me."

"Margo? The woman you used to work with? Did she ask you to have drinks again?"

"Not exactly. She asked me if I'd be interested in applying for a job with the D.A.'s office back in Portland."

"How did she take it when you said no?"

"I didn't exactly say no."

His head snapped so fast to look at her, she thought he was courting whiplash. "Why the hell not? You'd never consider going back to Portland." It was a statement, not a question.

"I don't know. Maybe I would."

"Seriously? After what you've told me about how you were treated? I can't believe it."

"I couldn't believe my reaction myself. But something inside my head kept jumping up and down saying, 'yes, now they see how good you are.' It would be a chance to show what a valuable asset I was, not some fuck-up."

"You've proved yourself time and time again here. Haven't you moved beyond needing to prove yourself to them?"

"I thought I had. I guess I haven't."

He stopped in the middle of the sidewalk. They were between streetlights, so his face was in shadow, and she couldn't read his expression, but the tone of his voice made it obvious he wasn't happy. "And what about us? I was hoping we had a future together."

"I hope we do, too."

"How're we going to make a future work when you're at one end of the state and I'm at the other?"

"You wouldn't consider moving back to Portland, then?"

"And do what? I can't pack up and leave the job I've been in for less than a year. Not after I lobbied to get it. I can't believe you're seriously asking me to do that so you can show people you haven't seen or heard from in over a year how right you were. That's not what the Juliet I know would ask. At least, I didn't think so."

Not sure what to say, she started walking slowly again, waiting for him to catch up. It took him a moment or two to start. When he was beside her again, she reached for his hand. He didn't push her away but he certainly didn't give her hand an affectionate squeeze, as he usually did.

"You're angry with me."

"I wouldn't say I'm angry. I'm surprised. Maybe disappointed. Okay, maybe a little angry." He dropped her hand and ran his fingers through his hair. "Jesus, Juliet, what did you expect I'd do? Jump up and down at the prospect of losing you to a job you said caused you so much embarrassment and regret that you ran away from it? Even if I got past that, how the hell do you think we'll carry on a relationship when you're in a life-sucking job in Portland and I'm in a pretty intense job five hours away in Ashland?"

"If we wanted to make it work, we could."

"How? With once-a-month conjugal visits in a motel in Cottage Grove? Meeting halfway between Portland and Ashland for sex and dinner isn't what I had in mind for our future. Is that what you'd settle for?"

"You're making this into something huge long before I've even decided what I'm going to do about it."

"Oh, you've decided, all right. You decided the minute you didn't tell her there was no way in hell you'd ever consider going back to Portland. That you have a good life here."

By this time, they'd reached her house. She started up the steps to her porch, but Trace hesitated. "You're not coming in tonight, are you?" she said, although she knew the answer already.

After a long pause, he said, "No, I think we both need to think this through. I'll call you tomorrow and we can talk."

If she'd hoped for a change of heart or a backward glance, he disappointed her.

His words weighed on her like a sixty-pound pack as she climbed the stairs to her bedroom. A few tears fell as she undressed for bed. More made their way down her face as she brushed her teeth. Once in bed, all she could see was the shocked look on his face when she'd told him she hadn't immediately rejected Margo's idea.

She and Trace had disagreed a few times about where to go for dinner or which movie to see, but they'd never had a serious argument. Well, assuming you didn't count the night he'd come to her house with her Juliet mask and she had thought he was trying to pull something sneaky. But this was worse. It was the first weekend since they'd begun seeing each other that she'd be alone. The first weekend they wouldn't fall asleep in each other's arms after making love. The first weekend without kisses and laughter and the feeling she was cared for. And not at all the way she'd expected to celebrate her birthday.

All because Margo Keyes had come to Ashland. If Margo had stayed home, no one in Portland would know where Julie was, and she'd be going on with her new life in Ashland as she had for over a year. But Margo had wanted to see a play, and everything had changed.

Chapter 14

Trace and Julie didn't talk on Sunday. He called and left a voice mail while she was out running. She didn't call back, not sure what there was to say until she knew what she was going to do about Portland. And she hadn't decided.

On Monday she got a call, but it wasn't from Trace.

Heather passed her a note as Julie was winding up a conference call. The note read, "There's a caller on line one who's very insistent."

Julie scribbled, "Take a message."

Heather wrote back, "He says he'll wait."

Julie gave her a questioning look and mouthed, "Name?"

"Jeff Wyatt," Heather wrote.

Julie's blood pressure spiked. She signaled she'd be finished in five minutes. Heather nodded and left.

In even less time, Julie was off her call and trying to calm her pounding heartbeat before she talked to Jeff. When she was as settled as she could be, she took the call.

"Hi, Jeff, sorry to keep you waiting. I was on a conference call."

"Your paralegal told me. Not to worry, Greer … uh … sorry. Margo says you're using your first name now. But I've forgotten what it is."

"It's Juliet—Julie around here. What can I do for you?"

"I think you already know. Margo told you we need someone with your abilities in the office, and I thought why look for a copy if we can have the original?"

"Why would you consider me when you told me what I'd done was a career-limiting move?"

"In the short run. I said it was career-limiting in the short run."

"I don't remember that part."

"Well, I do. The important point is, it's not the short run now, and there's a place for you here. Listen, I know how tough it was for you after Dreier was arrested. I even understand why you felt you had to leave. But now you've had your sabbatical. It's time to get back in the game. Is a solo practice in a small town drawing up wills really enough for you?"

Choosing her words carefully she said, "I have a rewarding practice here. It's not as boring as you make it sound. I'm busy and doing positive, helpful work."

"Yes, I'm sure you are. But you were one of my best deputies in court, and I'm betting you don't have much court time in Ashland."

He'd found her weak spot, and he knew it. She'd loved nothing more than going to court and winning. Which she almost always had.

"Would you consider coming up to Portland and talking to me in person?" he asked. After a second or two, when she didn't answer, he added, "Please?"

Julie had never heard Jeff say please in such a beseeching tone. Actually she wasn't sure she'd ever heard him say please at all.

She didn't answer right away. Memories of how humiliated she'd been, the questions from the Portland police, the embarrassing interviews with the FBI, all came back in force. The expressions on the faces of the colleagues who wouldn't meet her eyes when she returned from those sessions were burned into her memory. As were the details of the cases she'd been working on that had been suddenly reassigned to other people.

Mostly she remembered the session she'd had with the man at the other end of this phone call about what to expect because of her association with someone who'd be spending much of the rest of his life in prison.

But now that same person was coming to her, wanting her to return. There was enough of the old Greer left in the new Julie to gloat a little bit. And be tempted.

Finally she replied, "I guess it wouldn't hurt to talk to you about it. When would you like me to come up to Portland?"

"Later this week, maybe? Let me look at my calendar." There was the sound of papers shuffling. "I'm pretty open on Thursday morning if it works for you. Maybe you could spend the weekend, see some friends."

"I'll come up on Wednesday night and see you Thursday morning. I'll drive back right afterwards. I have plans for the weekend." *I hope.*

"Then let's make it breakfast at seven so you can get back to Ashland before it's dark. You remember how to find the Bijou?"

"I'm sure it'll come back to me."

"See you on Thursday. And thanks, Gr … uh … Julie."

She hung up wondering how she was going to tell Trace.

• • •

Deciding it was better to confront him at work, where there'd be no chance he'd lose it in front of his employees, she went to the bank right after lunch. He ushered her into his office and closed the door. He looked wary, as if unsure of what she would say.

"I was worried when you didn't call back yesterday." He directed her to a chair on one side of his desk and returned to his seat on the other.

"I didn't know what to say, so I didn't call."

He cocked his head and squinted one eye. "But somehow, now you know what to say?"

"Yes. At least, I know what to say about what I'm going to do in the short run." In a soft but determined voice she said, "I'm going to Portland on Wednesday for a Thursday morning breakfast with Jeff Wyatt, the D.A. He called this morning and asked me to come talk to him."

Trace leaned back in his chair, steepled his fingers, and put the tips of them up against his nose. The effect was to hide much of his expression from her, although she could still see his eyes, and they didn't look happy.

"I see."

"No, Trace, I don't think you do see. I need to close out that part of my life. I don't know yet if it means going back to work in the D.A.'s office. But I do know I have to figure it out. And going to talk with Jeff is the first step."

"And what about us?"

"Do you think you won't be an important part of figuring it out? Of course you'll be. All I'm asking right now is for you to cut me a little slack. I know this isn't easy for you, but it isn't easy for me, either. Nothing related to that part of my life has been easy for a long time now."

"Why can't you let it go? It's over, done." He dropped his hands onto the desk. The expression on his face made her heart ache. He was hurt; he was confused. He was probably still a little angry.

"I want to let it go, believe me. But it won't let go of me." She leaned onto the desk. "I don't know why it matters so much, but it does. It's like an itch I need to scratch or I'll go crazy. Please, can you bear with me for a week or two while I sort this out?"

She could see a series of expressions wash over his face. First a frown, then a puzzled look. Finally, a softening of the twitching muscle in his jaw, then a rueful smile. "I'm being a selfish dick, aren't I, thinking about myself instead of you. My only excuse is the whole thing came out of nowhere and knocked me sideways. Not much different from the way it hit you, I guess. I'm sorry."

He reached across the desk for her hands. "You have to figure out what you want. Then we'll go from there. What can I do, other than behave more like someone who wants what's best for you? Do you want company on the drive up on Wednesday? I have some business in Portland I could do in person rather than by phone and email."

"Tempting, but I think the time driving up and back will give me a chance to think everything through."

She got up, walked to the other side of the desk, and kissed him gently. "Will you have dinner with me before Wednesday?"

"Is that code for 'can I seduce you some night this week?'" he asked as he took her hands again.

"Well, it was an invitation for dinner at my house, but if we ended up in bed, I wouldn't mind."

"How about tonight?" He kissed the tips of her fingers. "I missed you this weekend."

"I missed you, too. I have a light afternoon, so I'll be home by four. Come when you want."

He raised an eyebrow. "That's the plan."

• • •

For the rest of the day, Trace was only able to get the basics done. He signed off on the pay records for the month, took all his incoming phone calls, returned calls, and answered emails. But the strategic plan he was working on couldn't keep his attention for more than a half hour, the speech he was supposed to give at the Chamber luncheon next week, even less. It was the least productive day he'd had since he'd arrived in Ashland.

He couldn't get out of his head what was now the very real possibility Julie would return to Portland permanently so she could put the ghost of her past to rest. Just when he'd gotten over falling for her so fast and so hard it unnerved him, this had happened. He was on a ledge looking down, wondering how it would feel when he hit the sidewalk.

He knew she'd been devastated by her Portland experience. It shouldn't have surprised him she wanted to find a way to finally and forever put it behind her. And yet it had. It had knocked him off balance. Badly. She'd been so successful at making herself indispensible to the community here, he'd assumed her experience had been sufficient to fill the hole in her self-confidence. It clearly hadn't.

He'd thought she'd be content to stay in Ashland with him. But in truth, if he put himself in her place, would he do what he was asking her to do? Probably not. He would want to find a way to get back some of the dignity and sense of worth he'd lost, just as she did.

Understanding the significance of what she was going through, however, didn't make it any easier for him to accept what he believed would be the outcome of this decision: The woman he loved, yes, loved, dammit, would move almost 300 miles away.

She was asking for time and space to make up her mind. Of course he'd give it to her. And while she thought about a decision capable of changing both their lives, he'd keep his mouth shut and his feelings to himself. If he could.

Chapter 15

Julie planned the dinner menu as carefully as if it were their first date. She got a fresh bottle of the Scotch that Trace liked for Rob Roys, and the merlot he always ordered with red meat. For dinner, she would serve his favorite peppercorn steak, a Caesar salad, bread from the bakery they both liked, and for dessert, chocolate cupcakes from the same place. She didn't know if she was preparing a peace offering, a thank you, or the last meal she'd ever have with him. Because she wasn't really sure what the outcome of the evening would be.

In only a few days, she'd swung from expecting a declaration of love from him to considering leaving him so she could return to the rat race of the D.A.'s office. She didn't exactly know how it had happened. And if she couldn't figure it out, how the hell could she expect Trace to understand? He'd put a good face on it today in his office. But how would it be tonight? It was hard to believe it would be smooth and easy. There would be an elephant the size of … well, the size of an elephant … in the room with them. Even the best sex in the world, which she knew they were capable of having, wouldn't move the elephant back out into its natural habitat.

As much as she wanted to reassure him she'd turn the job down if it were offered to her, she wasn't sure she would; not sure she could. Until she'd talked to Margo at the theater, she hadn't realized how much the humiliation still stung. What was worse, she didn't know exactly what taking a job back in the D.A.'s office would get her. Vindication? Maybe. The chance to make amends? Could be. The opportunity to restore her professional reputation with her former colleagues to some level of respect unsullied by what had happened? Possibly.

She was still mulling it all over when the doorbell rang. After the usual "hello, beautiful" and a casual kiss, Trace mixed a pitcher of Rob Roys, and they went into the living room. A silence more awkward than the first time he was in her house ensued.

"How was …?" she began, as he said, "So, what did …?"

After a nervous laugh, she said, "We don't usually discuss the hacking issue but maybe tonight it would be a good idea to break our rule. It's a safe subject, at least."

He nodded. "There's really not much to report. The IT department in Portland has finished investigating every other branch to see if anything similar has happened. They came up dry. The problem is confined to Ashland. IT is looking at other possibilities now."

Julie looked up at the ceiling for a moment. "I wonder. The intellectual property thefts, the ones my … uh, boyfriend … acquaintance … whatever … was involved with, they weren't always done by hacking into computer systems, although some were."

"If not by hacking, how was the information stolen?"

"It was transferred to flash drives, CDs, external hard drives. Laptops were stolen. It seems there's an endless number of ways to access supposedly inaccessible information."

"Why wouldn't our IT guys think of that?"

"Maybe they have. Or maybe they've been so pressured to find out how the system was hacked, they haven't had a chance to look at anything else."

"I guess." He drained his glass. "I'll ask the head of IT. He wants to talk to me at the end of the week. I assume to give me a report on what he's found—or not found, as the case may be. I'll pass along what you suggested, and I'll let you know what he has to say."

The subject exhausted, the conversation ground to a halt again.

She got up from the couch. "Maybe I better go put the finishing touches on dinner. It should only take me about fifteen minutes."

"No hurry."

• • •

No hurry indeed. Trace was happy for the break. He needed time to collect himself before they sat down for dinner, when the conversation was sure to die again. Last week they'd had so many things to talk about, they couldn't stop. Tonight, when they'd tried to talk about something other than the business they had to deal with, the strain between them was only too obvious.

Maybe seeing her tonight hadn't been such a good idea after all. He'd hoped a quiet evening would get them back into the close relationship they'd established. But it didn't seem to be working. The whole job thing stood in the way of everything—making plans for the next month, the next week, hell, the next day. Everything he could think to bring up would hinge on what her plans were when—he was sure it wasn't *if*—she was offered the damn job.

He wanted to go with her to Portland, to have her undivided attention while they drove up and down I-5 so he could lobby her. Yes, it felt like he was lobbying an elected official. He'd done some of it in his career and was pretty good at it. He'd presented his best case for the action he'd wanted, highlighted what was in it for the official, and answered questions. When he had been lucky, they had paid attention to the merits. When he hadn't been, they had referred him to their campaign manager and waited to see what he had contributed.

She didn't need a campaign contribution, so that was out. Unfortunately. Which left him with only the option of convincing her of the merits of his arguments. Which he'd been unsuccessful at thus far.

Going back to Portland was the wrong decision for her, he knew. Or thought he knew. Maybe it was only the wrong decision for him. Was it really fair of him to try and talk her out of what she needed to get past what had happened? After all, he wasn't the one who felt humiliated by a misjudgment. She was. He knew if he were a better person, he'd let her go if she needed to go. But he wasn't sure he was that good a person.

He checked out the pitcher in the ice bucket and, when he saw there was quite a bit of the cocktail left, poured it all into his glass. The Rob Roy didn't have a chance to lose one degree of chill from the pitcher before he had it half gone. Luckily, he'd walked from his house to hers. Because at the rate he was going, he would be too impaired to drive.

But instead of clouding his thoughts, the alcohol seemed to clear them. There really was only one thing he could do. He had to tell her what it was before he left tonight.

. . .

An hour later, dinner was gone, a bottle of wine almost finished, coffee poured, and the silence back. They'd avoided eye contact during the meal and talked only about the food. Trace had no idea he could say, "Nice dinner," in so many different ways.

The time had come to 'fess up. He looked across the table at her, cleared his throat, and said, "Look," as she said the same thing.

"Ladies first," he said.

"I didn't think this would be so awkward tonight. I'm sorry," she began. "It's all my fault for being so up in the air about Portland."

"No," he said. "It's my fault for being clueless about what it meant to you."

"So, now we fight to see who's the most sorry?" She finally smiled for the first time all evening.

"I don't want to fight about anything. So, I've been thinking …" He stopped, played with the empty coffee cup, then looked her squarely in the eye. "I think we should stay out of each other's way for the next few days."

"You mean break up?"

He heard the squeak in her voice that meant she was afraid. "No, no. Not break up. Just not hang out together. I thought we could patch things up tonight; have dinner, be like we were. But talking to each other has been harder than it was the first time I came here."

"I know, but maybe if we …"

"Do what, beautiful? Spend more evenings like tonight?"

"It hasn't been the best evening together, I'll grant you."

"We can't make plans until you make up your mind about what you want to do. I can't seem to stop wanting to lock you in a room to keep you from going to Portland." He shook his head. "And the other thing I can't seem to do is keep from saying things like that."

From the shiny eyes looking back at him, he knew she was close to crying. "Please don't cry, Juliet. I don't want to make you cry. But I don't see how it's going to be any better than it's been tonight until we know what you're going to do."

"So, no weekend together?"

"Do you think it'll be any better than tonight was?"

Now the tears were running down her face. He went to her and pulled her up from the chair. Holding her, kissing her hair, he made comforting noises until she stopped crying.

She picked up the napkin and wiped her face. "I gather you don't think a long distance relationship would work."

"I don't know if we're far enough into this to make it work."

"I know a couple; one of them is a city attorney in Oregon, the other one got a job about three years ago in Seattle. They make it work."

He took a handkerchief out of his pocket and cleaned up the raccoon eyes she'd gotten from smeared mascara as he asked, "Are they married?"

"Uh-huh. For five years."

"See, that I can understand. You build a good relationship over time and nothing can tear it apart. But we've only had months, not years."

She sighed. "I don't know what to say except I'll do whatever it takes to make it work out between us."

"I want to do that, too. But I need a breather so I can get prepared for whatever you're going to do."

"I guess this means you're not staying tonight."

He kissed her cheek. "I don't think so. I have an early breakfast meeting tomorrow and probably wouldn't have stayed anyway."

"Does this mean I won't see you at all? Talk to you?"

"I don't know what it means. I'll probably miss you so damn much I'll cave tomorrow."

"I hope so."

Chapter 16

In spite of Julie's hopes, Trace didn't cave after their Monday night dinner and ask to see her, although he did call on Wednesday to wish her a safe trip. The conversation was brief and a little reserved, much as the conversation at dinner had been. On Thursday she left for Portland with a Trace-size hole in her life she couldn't do anything about filling.

Her determination to use the time it took to drive to Portland to sort out what she'd do if the job were offered to her was thwarted. Idiots driving their vehicles too fast for the wet roads, and triple-trailer trucks boxing her in while trying to pass one another, made it impossible to do anything but pay strict attention to her driving. She arrived at the Marriott no more set on a decision than she'd been when she'd left Ashland.

The next morning she left the hotel early, making her way to the Bijou Café, enjoying being back in the city again. She'd always appreciated Portland's quirkiness. The town was a gracious, if somewhat weird, old lady among cities. Julie wondered what it would be like to return. Would she quickly settle back into urban rhythms, or would she miss the small-town life of Ashland? It was yet another question for her to think about.

She was early for their meeting, but Jeff Wyatt had gotten there even earlier, if the evidence of a *Wall Street Journal* in pieces on the table and a half-empty cup of coffee in front of him were to be believed. He rose when she approached the table and extended his hand.

"Greer … sorry … Julie, good to see you."

"Thanks, Jeff. It's good to see you, too. It's good to be back in Portland again."

"You look well. Happy. Relaxed. Your time in Ashland has agreed with you."

"It's been a good year. Very good." *Dear God, what's with the "goods?" I'm supposed to be good with words ... oh, fuck. Is it possible to be any more nervous? No, probably not.*

The server appeared and asked if they were ready to order. Julie asked for her favorite with no need to look at the menu—a cheese omelet, OJ, and coffee. Once Jeff had ordered, he leaned onto the table and asked, "So, tell me about your practice."

She told him about the business clients she'd served, the couple of scammers preying on seniors she'd gotten information on so the D.A. could prosecute, and the bank fraud clients. As she went on, she heard the pride in her voice about what she'd accomplished, felt the satisfaction she got from helping her clients. Her practice had become that important to her.

"You sound as if you really like it. I'm surprised. You always relished going to court to beat on the bad guys."

The server interrupted with their breakfasts. When he left, Julie responded. "Yes, I did like going to court. And I've done very little of it—really none at all—since I've been in Ashland. I miss it sometimes."

"Margo tells me you have a new man in your life."

"Yeah, I met him the first day he was in town, when I went to his office to tell him I was going to sue him." The real circumstances under which she'd met Trace made a better story but it wasn't one she planned to share with too many people. Jeff Wyatt certainly didn't make the cut for that list.

He laughed. "There's the Greer I know. Even if she is Julie these days."

"It's not the way most relationships begin, but it seems to have worked for us."

"From the sound of your voice when you talk about it, you're happy with your practice. You have a new boyfriend. You've liked living in Ashland. So, why are you sitting across the table from me in Portland talking about an opening in my office?"

Momentarily stunned, Julie took a few seconds to recover. "You asked to see me."

"And you didn't say 'no, thanks' when I asked," he said softly. "I'm wondering why."

There, in a nutshell, was what made Jeff so good at what he did. *Damn, there was that word again.*

"I didn't think it would hurt to see what my options were. Maybe you'll make me an offer I can't refuse."

"A Godfather reference. Hmm. Not sure what to think of that." He finished off his second cup of coffee, pushed his now-empty plate away, and lounged back in his chair. "You know what I have to offer. Long hours and plenty of stress, a decent but not great salary, and the best office furniture the county could afford in the nineteen-eighties. Then there's the good stuff—the chance to make a real difference in the world, to nail the bastards who need nailing, and the opportunity to do it all in a very public and sometimes spectacular way. The question is, are you interested?"

"Honestly? I'm not sure."

"Tell me why you decided to come talk to me."

"Part of it is what you said before—I sometimes miss the challenge of arguing a court case. I loved the work I did for you. It was exciting, rewarding." She fiddled with the spoon on her saucer. "But mostly I'm here because it seems I haven't gotten past how it ended. I know I made a huge mistake in judgment with Paul, but I didn't think—don't think—I deserved to be treated like a pariah after it all ended."

"I'm sorry you felt that way. It wasn't anyone's intention—certainly not mine—to make you feel like an outcast."

"Whatever the intentions were, it's how it came across. And why part of me looks at this as a chance to redeem myself. To let go of what happened, so I can get on with my life."

"If I offer you the job, will you stick around after you feel you've found what you're looking for, or will you take off again for parts unknown?"

"*If* I'm offered it and *if* I take it, I'll be as committed as I was when I worked for you before. You have my word on it."

He looked at her long and hard. "Then we understand each other. I'd like you to think about this seriously. And I will, too. I have two other candidates to interview and I should be able to make a decision by next week. You have until then to decide what you want."

He waved to the server for the bill. "I think—I *know*—you'd be an asset to the office. The question is, can we still give you what you want for your professional life? Only you have the answer." He threw down a credit card and added, "Now I have to get to work. Busy day. As usual."

Surely her surprise showed on her face. "That's the interview? Don't I have to give you a résumé or go back to the office with you so you can, I don't know, ask me about … something?"

Jeff laughed. "I can get your personnel file if I need to remind myself where you went to law school, and I assume you're still a member in good standing with the Oregon bar. I wanted two things out of this meeting. One, to let you know face-to-face how serious I am about considering you for this opening and, two, to find out how interested you are. I hope I've done the first, and you've certainly been honest about the second."

He signed the credit card receipt and stood. "But if you want to walk back to the office with me, you might see how comfortable you'd be back where I think you belong. And I'm sure Margo would like to see you. She said she didn't have much time to catch up with you in Ashland. Although I have to say, the details on how you looked and who you were with were quite complete."

"She's always been good at details."

That's it. An embargo on the word good. For the day at least. Maybe for the month.

• • •

The last time Julie had been in the courthouse, she'd been sur-reptitiously boxing up her personal things, so she could sneak out without anyone noticing. Today, thanks to Margo Keyes, who saw her as soon as she walked in, she couldn't avoid attention.

After an hour or so of what were, to Julie's surprise, comfortable conversations with a dozen or more people, Margo chased everyone out of her office and said, "How about a cup of coffee someplace outside the building where we can have a little privacy and talk?"

As soon as they settled in the nearest Starbucks, Margo broke the ice. "I'm sure you told Jeff everything about your practice in Ashland, so we don't have to go over the subject again—I'll dig it out of him later. Tell me about Trey."

"It's Trace. And what's to tell? He's the bank manager for the Northwest Savings and Loan branch in town. He's smart, fun to be with …"

"Sexy as hell from the look of him. How did you meet him?"

"In an unusual way, I guess you can say. I was representing a group of clients suing his bank." She was tempted to tell Margo the truth, to explain about meeting him in costume, about dumping hot coffee on him. It was the sort of story a woman shared with her female friends. Or a woman she'd like to have for a friend.

But Julie knew Margo and Jeff might talk, might compare notes. And if she was going to work in that office again, she had to be careful who knew about the unorthodox way she'd met Trace. The last thing she needed was to have them think she still had bad judgment when it came to men.

"So you're saying you threatened to sue him, and he fell for you?"

Julie laughed. "It was a little more complicated, but it's close."

"If it's as good between you two as it looked when I saw you in the theater, why would you ever leave town?"

"I haven't decided yet whether I am leaving town. First, the job hasn't been offered to me. Second, I don't know if I'll accept it."

"Better work on the answer to the second part, because I'd be shocked if you weren't offered the job. The other two candidates are good lawyers, but neither has your skill or experience. One hasn't ever worked in a D.A.'s office, but has handled cases involving fraud. The other doesn't know shit about fraud, but is smart and has worked in a D.A.'s office in Washington State. Jeff would rather have it all in one person so he doesn't have to be a babysitter through the first couple years."

Julie fidgeted in her seat. "I've been driving Trace nuts with my indecision. He's used to giving orders and having people do what he says. This in-between stuff isn't his style."

"Giving orders? Even to you? You're not exactly the type I'd imagine following them too easily." Margo cocked her head and pursed her mouth. "Unless, of course, you like the orders he's giving." She took a sip of her coffee and almost spit it out when she looked across the table. "Oh, my God, you're blushing. I've never seen you blush. He must be one hell of a man to …"

"Can we move to another topic, please? This is getting too embarrassing."

"Sure. What would you like to talk about other than your hot guy who makes you obey him?"

"Jesus, Margo. Now I'm glad I never got into girly chats with you before. You're terrible."

"No, according to my husband, I'm funny and cute. At least that's how he describes me when I do the same thing to him."

"How *is* the gorgeous Detective Alessandro?"

"Fine. He loves his job. Has started riding a bike, can you believe, after years of only riding a motorcycle. Oh, and we're pregnant."

"Wow. Congratulations." Julie raised her coffee cup in a toast. "You don't look it."

"I'm only three months. We've just started to tell people about the rather large change in our lives that will arrive in six months."

"Whether it's a boy or a girl, with you two for parents, you'll have a smart, beautiful child." Julie's mind wandered briefly to what a baby she and Trace created would be like. She shook her head to get the thought out of it.

Margo's phone buzzed. She looked at it, then said, "Text from Kiki reminding me about a deposition. Time for me to get back to the courthouse. Before I do, let me stick my nose in where it doesn't belong. As much as I want you to come back to Portland so we can start over with knowing each other, please don't make this decision based on some idea of proving something to the office. You don't need to prove a damn thing to anyone. You deserve to be happy now, not stuck in the past. And believe me, you sure looked happy with Trace."

"I am. And I'll think about what you said. I promise. It means a lot coming from you."

The two women stood, and Margo hugged Julie hard and long. This time Julie hugged her back. She kept one hand on Margo's shoulder, paused for a moment, then continued. "You know, I never really thanked you for what you did two years ago. In spite of the fact we weren't close, you stuck up for me. Even helped me in those awful interrogations with the police and the FBI. So, though it's a little late, thank you."

"You did thank me. And I didn't do anything other than make sure you had every right you were entitled to. It's what lawyers do, I hear."

"No, you did more than protect my rights. You offered me your support when everyone else turned away from me." Julie smiled. "I'd say I'd return the favor, but I don't think you'll ever need it."

"You never know. I hear pregnancy hormones are a bitch. I might snap, and who knows what I'll do? Maybe you should give me your card, just in case."

Chapter 17

At least the drive back to Ashland was less cluttered with trucks, stupid drivers, and wet roads than the drive up to Portland had been. Unfortunately, even with dry roads, five hours wasn't long enough to get anything resolved. In fact, Julie was more confused than ever. She'd been happy to be back in Portland but was excited when she saw the sign announcing Ashland was one exit away. She'd enjoyed talking with Margo and wanted to take her up on her offer to start over with their friendship. On the other hand, she could hardly wait to talk with her book club about the great book she'd finished during her hotel stay and to find out from her theater friends how the season was shaping up for the Festival.

And then the big one: she was almost ecstatic that Jeff might want her back, but horrified at the idea of leaving Trace.

It was almost dark by the time she got home. She was tired. She was wrung out by the events of the past week. All she wanted to do was crawl into bed. Preferably with Trace, but she didn't think the option was on the table.

It wasn't until she was unlocking her front door that she saw the vase of stargazer lilies sitting in the shadows. She didn't have to guess who left them—she recognized Trace's handwriting on the envelope tucked in the greenery around the flowers. The note inside said, *Welcome home, beautiful. Hope your trip was everything you wanted it to be. Call me and let me know you got back safely. Love, Trace.*

She didn't unpack, freshen up, or think twice. She called him.

"Hi, I'm home. Thank you for the lovely flowers."

"You're welcome. Glad they didn't get stolen. You have a good trip?"

"It was great. I loved seeing Portland again. Had a good breakfast meeting with Jeff, then talked to a bunch of people in the office and wound up having coffee with Margo before I came back home."

There was another of those pesky silences for a few moments. "So you'll get the job offer."

"Margo thinks I will. But I told both Margo and Jeff I didn't know if I'd accept the job if it was offered to me."

"Still don't know, huh?"

"No, haven't figured it out." She was reluctant to ask the question that had played around the edges of everything she'd thought about all the way home, not sure she could face one of the alternative answers. But if she didn't ask, she had no chance of getting the answer she wanted to hear. So she said, "Since I haven't made up my mind yet, do you still want us to avoid each other?"

He groaned. "Jesus, Juliet, I don't know how much longer I can go without seeing you. You have no idea how much I miss you."

"I hope it's as much as I miss you. Please, Trace, can't we take a break from taking a break? I need to see you. I've never begged a man for anything in my life but I'm begging you. Can I see you tonight?"

"I'm on my way."

•••

He'd left her favorite flowers so she'd call. And hoped when she did, she'd ask to see him. He knew he'd go if she asked. Now he was halfway to her house wearing only a light jacket over ragged jeans and an old sweatshirt. Eager to see her, he hadn't taken the time to change into something nicer or find a warmer coat against the cold. Although why he was worried about what he was wearing he couldn't say. Especially since he hoped to be out of them at the first opportunity. Maybe it was easier worrying about clothes than it was to worry about what she would say when he got there. And whether he'd get that opportunity.

He'd realized during his self-imposed withdrawal from her that he couldn't protect himself from being deeply wounded if she accepted the job in Portland, no matter what he did. It was also obvious he couldn't ask her to pick him over finding her way to whatever resolution she needed about the past.

The upshot was, he would spend as much time with her as he could, as she'd let him, and hope for the best.

Her porch light was on and the door slightly ajar. He didn't bother to knock. She didn't bother to say hello when he walked in. They collided in the middle of the living room and immediately locked mouths. Teeth bumped, lips devoured, arms tightened, bodies melded. His mouth demanded what she was only too willing to give freely—desire, need, passion.

"I need you," he whispered. "God, how I need you. Let's go upstairs."

"No. Too far. I don't want to wait that long."

She pulled him back to the couch, and he slid her skirt up so it was bunched around her waist. He pushed her thong down around her ankles so she could step out of it, and laid her down. Dressed now in a thin camisole and a belt made of her suit skirt, she was on her back on the couch as he unzipped and shed his jeans and boxers, pulled a condom out of his pocket, and knelt between her legs. Saying, "I've never wanted anyone the way I want you," he ripped open the foil packet and covered himself.

Then he was over her, pressing his erection against her sex as he kissed her and kissed her and kissed her. He couldn't get enough of her mouth. Couldn't stop massaging and molding her breasts under the camisole. Couldn't stop pulling her hips up against him. Finally, couldn't keep from thrusting into her, where she was wet and ready for him.

...

It was like she imagined the middle of a tornado was—breathtaking, fast, and exhilarating, potentially dangerous. She'd never had anyone kiss her with so much desire. She'd never felt her body go liquid so quickly. Never wanted anyone inside her so badly. The feelings were overwhelming. Trace was overwhelming. And he was everything she wanted.

It didn't take long to get what they both wanted. He collapsed on her, as exhausted from his climax as she was from hers. All she could do was hold him close and wonder how she had ever believed she was alive before she met him.

He raised his head and touched his sweaty forehead to hers. "Jesus, I don't know what happened. I've never behaved like that before. I didn't hurt you, did I?" He started to roll off the couch, but she wouldn't let him.

"Of course not." She touched a finger to his mouth, then kissed where she had touched. "We seem to do a lot of things neither one of us has done before, don't we? I can honestly say, for example, I've never had sex on this couch before."

The smile she got in response was sweet. "Maybe we should work up a list of other pieces of furniture like the couch and, you know, check them off."

"Making a list and checking it? I don't need a list to tell you who's naughty."

She moved under him to get the edge of the couch cushion in a more comfortable place on her back. He reacted by rising onto his forearms. "I'm not quite the size of Santa, but I must be hurting you now. This space is even more cramped than your bed is." He leveraged himself to his knees, then off the couch, grabbed his jeans, and headed for the downstairs powder room. "Don't go away; I'll be right back."

By the time he returned, she'd gotten dressed herself, except for her thong, which was AWOL, and had poured two glasses of wine.

He took the glass she offered him, winked, and said, "I don't know if this is such a good idea. God knows what I'll do with a little alcohol in me." But he took a sip anyway.

Now it was her turn to smile and wink. "I didn't expect you to agree so easily to seeing me tonight. But maybe I have the answer now. It's not that I was so persuasive; it's because you were ready to call off the calling off."

He shook his head. "The dumbest thing I've ever done was try and stay away from you to insulate myself against missing you if you decide to leave. I was a fool. And I lost almost five days with you because of it." Putting his arms around her, he concluded with, "Forgive me."

"I've had a hard time this week not seeing you."

"Then let's make up for it. Let me take you to dinner."

"No, dinner here. I don't want to share you. Let me change, and I'll make something."

He glanced up and down her body. "Be prepared for what you see when you take off your skirt. I made a mess of it. I'll take it to the dry cleaner."

"The hell you will. First time on the couch. First time in this suit—well, part of this suit. I might frame it. This I can frame, the couch I can't."

• • •

The weekend following her return from Portland made up a bit for what they had missed being apart. At Trace's insistence, they left Friday after work for the coast. It was another long drive for Julie, but it was worth it when they got there. They walked on the beach and watched the winter storm-tossed waves, explored new restaurants, found a theater playing a movie they hadn't seen. In short, acted like any other couple on a get-away weekend. Not once did either one say anything about the decision Julie had to make. Although it wasn't very far from her consciousness all weekend, she managed to keep it from pushing its way into the conversation. She didn't know how Trace managed to stop thinking about it. Maybe he didn't. What she did know was he didn't bring it up.

The beginning of the workweek came too soon for either of them.

Wanting to keep the weekend glow going, they snuck in coffee together Monday morning and talked about plans for the coming weekend, as they'd been doing for months.

Shortly after they parted with a quick kiss in front of the coffee shop, she got a call on her cell. Trace.

"Can't live without me after only a few minutes?" she said when she picked up.

"Juliet, I have some information about your clients' problems I think you'll be interested in." He was all business in spite of calling her on her cell and not her office phone.

"Okay. Do you want to come here, or should I come to you?"

"I'd like you to bring as many of your clients as you can round up to the bank tomorrow at two. I have three home office officials coming down from Portland to meet with us then."

"Can you give me a hint what this is about so I can pass it on to my clients?"

"All I can tell you is we may have resolution to the problem."

"All you can tell me, or all you know?"

His laugh finally moved the conversation from the stiff and formal to the personal. "You know me too well. It's all I know. My boss says they want to make the announcement to everyone, including bank staff here, at the same time."

Chapter 18

It took Julie and Heather the rest of the day to get the entire client group notified about the meeting with the bank officials. Not everyone was able to attend, but on Tuesday afternoon, about twenty people were crowded into the bank's largest conference room well in advance of the appointment time. Promptly at two, Trace and three other people walked in: a tall, middle-aged, African-American man; an older, white-haired man; and a dark-haired woman. The woman's well-tailored, going-to-court suit, her low-heeled shoes, and her serious looking hairstyle made Julie believe she was looking at a fellow attorney.

Trace began, "Thank you all for coming here on what was short notice. I have three people with me from our home office in Portland. Let me first introduce the man who's going to run the meeting." He indicated the African-American man. "This is Jonathon Monroe, the head of the bank's information technology department. With him is Emma Jacobs, from the legal department, and Henry Alexander, the man I report to. Jon, why don't I sit down and shut up so these folks can hear from you." And he did.

Clearly amused by his introduction, Monroe looked around the room, a slight smile on his lips. "Thanks, Trace. Always glad to work with someone who wants to get down to business without a lot of preliminaries. And with a group of people who are motivated enough to move their schedules around to be here."

From the back of the room came a *sotto voce* comment from one of the seniors. "Damn straight we're motivated. It's our money that was stolen."

"And that's why I'm here," Monroe said. "We've spent a lot of time chasing ghosts trying to figure this out. Two different firms specializing in protecting companies from computer hacking have been over our system, at all our branches, with a fine-tooth comb. They found no indications of any hacking anywhere. Ever. They assured us we have one of the best computer security systems in the business. They did a couple updates while they were in there looking around, but they turned up nothing to help us identify what was going on here in Ashland. And only in Ashland."

A few hands went up; a whole lot of questions were shouted out by other people not willing to wait to be recognized. Monroe held up his hand like a flagger on a road construction project and said, "Please. If you'll hold your questions until I'm finished, I'd appreciate it. I think what I'm about to say might answer a lot of them." Julie added a stern look to his suggestion, focused on one or two of her most irritating clients. The hands went down and the noise level followed, albeit reluctantly and with grumbling from more than a few people.

"After we'd done the Sherlock Holmes thing of eliminating the obvious answers first, we started looking for other ways the information could have been stolen. Trace tells me your attorney Ms. Payne has experience in this area, and he relayed a couple suggestions she made that tracked with what we were already beginning to look at. So we were all on the same page."

"What page was it?" one of the students asked.

"It came down to two possibilities—a bank computer with the information was stolen, or the information itself was transferred onto something and removed from the bank." Monroe was pacing the floor at this point, focused more on what he was saying than on his audience.

"We'd already eliminated the stolen computer possibility. No computers—laptop or desktop—were missing from this branch. Not now. Not for the past few years. When computers were replaced, the hard drives were destroyed according to bank policy. So that wasn't it."

He stopped and looked out at the group. "Then we looked for who would be able to transfer the information onto something and walk out with it. Not very many people have access to all the right information plus the skills to send out the phishing letters and malware to the account holders."

"So," Trace asked, "who dunnit?"

Monroe looked at his watch. "I'm expecting someone in a few minutes who'll answer that question," he said.

Julie, who was sure the IT head was enjoying this performance, raised her hand. When he recognized her, she asked, "If you won't tell us who yet, will you tell us how?"

"We were looking for flash drives or an external hard drive taken to a home computer. We found computer traces of suspicious downloads, along with the times and the login of the probable perpetrator once we started looking for that instead of a hacker."

"Why didn't the guy Clyde Lindstrom hired find the same information you did?" Trace asked.

Before Monroe could answer the question, there was a knock at the door. Everyone stopped talking. Julie was almost convinced everyone had stopped breathing while Trace went to the door and opened it.

To the visible surprise of everyone except the three Portland bank people, Clyde Lindstrom was standing there.

Henry Alexander waved him into the room. "Please, join us, Clyde."

Julie saw the man she'd known as a responsible banker and stand-up member of the community scan the room, his eyes resting here and there on specific people. With every face he seemed to recognize, he grew paler, his breath became more labored.

"What's all this?" Lindstrom asked. "I was told I was to meet with someone from the home office. Something about my retirement."

Jonathon Monroe introduced himself, adding, "Which is exactly what we're here to discuss, Mister Lindstrom. Or more accurately, your future. Please, sit down next to Mister Watkins."

Turning away from the now chalk-white and sweating Clyde Lindstrom, Monroe addressed the group in front of him. "Unfortunately, here is the source of all your—and our—problems. Our former bank manager, Clyde Lindstrom."

"What the hell are you talking about? I never caused any problems," Lindstrom said.

Monroe continued as if he had not been interrupted. "Mister Lindstrom and, it turns out, his nephew, are quite skillful with computers. Between the two of them, they stole customers's account information, sent phony emails and malware to those customers, and, most important, took money from the accounts of some of the people in this room."

"This is all trumped up to get the bank off the hook because of their bad security system." Lindstrom's face was red with anger, his voice indignant. But Julie had enough experience with witnesses to know the indignation was a cover for fear. She could hear it in his voice. She could see it in the way he squirmed in his chair and wiped his hands on his pant legs as if to wipe off his sweaty palms—or his guilt.

"You may have tried to erase them, but we found enough traces of what you did to lead us to you. And we'll soon have more evidence," Monroe said to Lindstrom. "The Ashland police are now at your and your nephew's houses, removing computers and computer-related gear. And before you ask, yes, they have the warrants they need to do it."

Lindstrom stood and squared his shoulders. "I don't have to sit here and listen to this bullshit from a bunch of people who've shown no appreciation for what I contributed to the organization. Who forced me out in favor of some young punk who'd never even been to Ashland and doesn't know jack shit about the community. I'm leaving."

Emma Jacobs stood in his way. "You're not going anywhere, Mister Lindstrom. We have a lot of questions for you."

"I'm not saying anything without an attorney."

"That's your right." She looked like she was about to say something else, but Lindstrom interrupted.

Making a move toward Julie he said, "This is all your fault, you slut. You and the punk you've been sleeping with. If you hadn't …

Trace leapt to his feet and grabbed the collar of Lindstrom's shirt so tightly the older man couldn't finish his sentence. Only Jonathon Monroe's intervention kept Trace from what seemed to be his intention of punching the older man. Two other people sprang to Julie's defense—one senior from her client group and, surprisingly, the college student who had caused her so much heartburn by wanting to gouge the bank for all the money he could. They too went for Lindstrom but were restrained by others. Most of the rest of her clients gathered around her as if to form a protective shield. People were shouting. No one was still seated. It was a meeting gone completely out of control.

In the midst of the melee, a uniformed policeman stepped into the room. "Need assistance here?" he asked.

"I think we do, officer," Henry Alexander said.

The cop pounded his flashlight on the conference room table like a judge trying to gavel down unruly spectators. Everyone in the room froze in place like a stop-action frame in a cartoon. Fists were raised; mouths open. Shirts were clutched; fingers pointed.

"Now that I have your attention," the officer said, "I suggest we all calm down so I can do what I was sent to do. I'd like to walk away with only the person I was sent to arrest, not have to call for backup to cuff half the people here for causing a disturbance." Before he could get his flashlight back on his equipment belt, the room quieted, and most everyone took their seats.

The officer brought a pair of handcuffs from behind his back and approached Clyde Lindstrom. As he cuffed the former bank manager, the officer recited the familiar words of the Miranda warning.

In minutes, the officer and Lindstrom were gone. As those in the room continued to return to order, Trace came to Julie and knelt by her, took her hand, and kissed her knuckles. "You okay, Juliet?" he asked. He rubbed her arm as he spoke.

"I'm fine, thanks." She shrugged. "Sticks and stones, you know."

"He threw quite a pointed stick or a pretty large boulder at you, whichever you want to call it."

"He can't hurt me, Trace. Not now." She squeezed his hand. "We better get the meeting over. I imagine you and the folks from Portland have a lot to do before your day's over."

"Yeah. I'm afraid dinner tonight is off."

"I figured." She also figured half the room was eavesdropping on their conversation, so she let go of his hand and shooed him to the front of the room.

Jonathon Monroe stood. "So, as you can see, we think we have finally solved the mystery. It'll be up to the D.A. to see if we're right but I'm confident we have the evidence to successfully press charges." He paced the floor again as he was speaking, clearly pleased with himself and his people.

"From what we've pieced together, Clyde Lindstrom retrieved information on the bank's customers during the six weeks before he retired. While he was in and out of the office packing up his personal belongings, he may have been trying to get more information to use, although we think all the damage was done with information he collected while he was still working for the bank. He wouldn't have had access to any of the computers after he retired although he may have been trying to work around that system."

Julie raised her hand. "The nephew … what was his role?"

"He was the outside investigator whose report said nothing was wrong. And we suspect the nephew also had a hand in sending the malware. He's more of a computer geek than his uncle is, although Mr. Lindstrom knew his way around the bank's system thanks to the training courses we paid for him to attend." There were a few chuckles in the audience before Monroe continued. "We'll know more about it when we look through their home computers."

He looked around the room. "Any more questions about the IT end of this?" There were no hands up, only a room full of smiling people. "No? Good. Now I'll turn the meeting over to my legal colleague for her part of the story."

Emma Jacobs stood. "I won't take up too much of your time. I will contact Ms. Payne to work out the details of the settlement the bank will offer you. But here's the broad outline. We've already made whole everyone we know who lost money from an account at this branch. Once we have access to Mister Lindstrom's computer and can find out exactly what data he has, we'll be contacting any other people who may have been harmed as you were."

She pulled a document out of her briefcase. "I have here the list of whom we've reimbursed and when, which I'll leave with your attorney so she can review it and make sure we got everyone who was affected."

Walking over to Julie she handed her the papers. "One—no, two—last things. I'll be negotiating a settlement with Ms. Payne to offer you compensation for your time and trouble, and to cover any expenses you may have had such as late fees, overdraft charges, or fees from bounced checks."

She had her hand on Julie's shoulder when she added, "Last, we are prepared to cover all your legal expenses."

From the back of the room came a loud, "Now's the time to raise your hourly rate, Julie." It was Julie's friend, Martha Combes, of course. The laughter following her suggestion relaxed everyone and ended Jacobs's presentation on a light note.

Trace ended the meeting as he'd begun it, with a short and to-the-point statement. "Thanks for your patience while we figured this out. It took longer than we'd hoped, but it's finally resolved. The four of us will be around for a while if you have any more questions."

The floodgates opened. Most of Julie's clients surrounded Trace and the three bank officials. The few who didn't hugged Julie, thanked her, and told her how invaluable she'd been in getting the problem taken care of. Emma Jacobs broke away from the scrum at the front of the room to thank Julie for the way she'd handled the case, and teasingly—or maybe not—said if she got tired of a private practice, she might consider working for the bank's legal department.

Julie waited for a few minutes to see if she could talk to the other two bank officials, but they were so busy with her clients asking questions, saying thanks or whatever, she couldn't get the attention of either of them. She couldn't even get Trace's attention. So she slipped out of the room.

She could barely control her urge to yell, "Yippee!" and do a happy dance as she walked along Main Street. They'd won. She'd won. It was the biggest success she'd had since she'd come to Ashland. This even felt better than the case she'd prosecuted a few years back—a man who'd run a multi-million dollar Ponzi scheme. The guy in Portland had targeted people who were wealthy, which didn't make their losses any less important, only less immediately threatening to their health and wellbeing. Her Ashland clients included many who had lost the money to pay for food or rent, who were not able to recover easily from even a $100 hit to their bank account.

It was time to celebrate. She had nothing else on her calendar, and it was close enough to the end of the business day, she felt no guilt about closing up shop. Walking along the street, she called her office to tell Heather the good news.

"Hey, you up for leaving early and having a glass of wine to celebrate?"

Heather squealed her joy. "We won? We really won?"

"You sound like Sally Field. Yes, we won, and they really love us. We got a good settlement for our clients and all our costs covered by the bank. I'm in the mood to buy my staff a glass of the best wine at her favorite bar."

"It'll have to be a quick one. Zane is taking me to meet his parents tonight."

Zane, with his Harley and nose ring, shaved head and tattooed neck, was her boyfriend. He was also a nurse practitioner, which always amazed Julie.

"Things are that serious, are they? Go home and take your time getting ready. We'll celebrate another time."

"Are you sure? I can have a quick drink now and still be ready by six."

"No, meeting the parents is much more important."

"Congratulations, Julie. You deserve a celebration. Maybe we should have another party."

Julie stifled a laugh, remembering the last time she'd followed that particular piece of advice. "We can talk about it in the morning. Good luck meeting the parents."

She made a few more phone calls only to discover her best woman friend was out of town. Several other friends weren't answering texts. The one she reached had a performance that night. With Trace tied up at the bank, she was out of people she wanted to celebrate with, so she went home. For the first time in her life, she wished she had a pet. At least a cat or dog would recognize someone who was in a good mood and would party along with her.

In the comfort of her home, she replayed the meeting. Relished the shout out she'd gotten from Jon Monroe, the professional respect Emma Jacobs had shown her—even a job offer, if only in fun. The response she'd gotten from her clients both after the meeting and when Clyde Lindstrom had insulted her. She'd had grateful victims thank her for putting away a bad guy before, but no one had ever ridden to her rescue quite the way it had happened today. And Trace. In front of his boss, her clients, and God, he'd defended her and claimed her as special.

Nothing she'd experienced compared with the events of this day.

The hell with it. Even if she was doing it alone, she was going to celebrate with dinner at her favorite restaurant.

She wasn't exactly alone while she ate. Several people who'd heard the news already stopped by her table to thank her for being so persistent in helping her clients. A bottle of pinot grigio and a serving of crème brûlée—her favorite wine and her favorite dessert—were sent to her table. It would have made Greer freak out to have so many people know what she liked, but it made Julie feel a part of her community.

Home by eight, the wave of adrenaline, burnt sugar, and wine she'd been riding subsided, and she was suddenly quite tired. She thought about pouring another glass of the wine from the bottle she'd brought home with her, but decided against it, stashing the almost-full bottle in the refrigerator instead. She flipped through the hundred or so movies on her Netflix queue and found nothing to interest her. Finally she gave up on television, took her Kindle to bed, and pulled up a mystery novel she hadn't read.

Chapter 19

The mystery novel was clearly well written, because when the phone rang at eleven, Julie was startled, both by the sound and the time.

It was Trace, yawning and apologizing for calling at the late hour.

"Don't apologize. I'm glad you called. You've had one hell of a day, haven't you?"

"Like no other in my career. I just got home. Between talking to the police, talking to the home office, and talking to each other, I think Henry, Jon, Emma and I used up every word in the English language today."

"What'd the cops find? Anything you can share?"

"There's still a lot of computer data to search, but from what they've found so far, Lindstrom and his nephew had hundreds more names and bank records, which Jon had already suspected, given what his people found."

"What's Lindstrom's motive? Did he say?"

"Oh, yeah, he's real clear about the reason and willing to tell anyone, everyone, with or without an attorney present. He's pissed off at bank management for what he says they did by forcing him into retirement and putting me into what he still thinks of as *his* job. He's rabid on the subject."

"A couple people tonight told me everyone knew he'd been a little off since his wife died," Julie said. "They'd been married since they were in college and about to celebrate a fiftieth anniversary when she died. But I don't think anyone had any idea he was this bad."

"No one at the bank knew, that's for sure," Trace said. "Although a couple people said they'd noticed he spent more time at work since she died. His world shrunk to the confines of his office, as one woman described it. She thought he hated going home alone to a house they'd shared for so long." He coughed, as if to cover up a tightening of his throat. "I guess I can understand. At least the part about missing someone you care about so much it hurts."

Now her throat tightened up. "Really?"

"Haven't you ever felt like that?"

"I think I have. Only recently, in fact."

"Yeah, me, too." Another cough and a pause before he led the conversation in another direction. "Anyway, that's about all the police will tell us. Except for one other thing. My personal bank accounts are frozen. Seems they found some evidence the nephew might have recently added malware to them. Not sure what it is set to do, but they think it might be either to automatically loot my accounts or to somehow make me look guilty of the other thefts."

"Frozen your accounts? How will you pay your bills? Buy food?"

"'Frozen' was probably a bad word choice. Most of the money from my checking account was transferred to a new account, but the old one was kept open to see what happens. The only problem is all the changes to my automatic payments I'll have to make, but I still have money. My savings account has been blocked from anyone having access to it, including me, until they work out what he's done. But thank you for worrying about me."

"Of course I worry about you. You're … well, you're whatever you are to me."

"There's the explanation of a woman's feelings I've always wanted to hear."

"I know. Bad, huh?"

"It's okay. I know how you feel."

Now it was Juliet's turn to change the subject. "What will the bank have to do to clean this up?"

After a few silent moments during which she was afraid he might go back to the sticky subject of how they felt about each other, he said, "It's gonna be hell. Outside auditors will come in and go through almost everything Lindstrom ever did. Then there's the PR aspect. We have to distance ourselves from him and make sure customers and potential customers understand he was a bad apple and our system is trustworthy. At the same time, we have to tread gently—he's a hometown boy even if he's also a hometown thief."

"And everyone knows how hard his wife's death hit him. How will you … what will you …?"

"I'm not exactly sure how or what. But it'll be up to me to regain the community's confidence."

"You already have everyone's trust."

"I hope it doesn't take too big a dent from this. I'll worry about it after we get a handle on how much mess we have to clean up." He yawned again. "I don't know when I've ever been this tired yet still so wound up."

"Would you like a shoulder rub?"

"What kind of masseuse makes house calls at this hour of the night?"

"Me, for one."

"As much as I'd love to have you come spend the night, I'm too tired for sex." Another yawn. "Jesus, did I just say that? I'm sure those words have never crossed my mind let alone my lips before. And I probably would chase you out even if I wasn't so tired. I have an early morning breakfast with Jon and Henry."

"A: there was no mention of sex. B: there was no mention of my staying overnight. C: the offer was for a shoulder rub to relax you enough so you can get some sleep before your next day from banking hell. D: …"

"I get it, Madam Attorney. I get it."

"Good, because there was no 'D.' I'd run out of exhibits for your consideration."

"If you come over, will I get to see what you wear to bed when I'm not around?"

"I'd planned to dress before I walked the streets at eleven, Trace. I'm not an idiot."

"Then tell me what you're wearing. I've always been curious."

"Is this headed toward phone sex because you're too tired for actual sex?"

"I think I'm even too tired for that. But I still want to know what you're wearing. Is that so perverted?"

"Maybe not *so* perverted, although it is a little."

There was a frustrated groan from the other end of the line.

"All right," she said. "If it's so important to you. I sleep in boy shorts and a camisole."

"That doesn't sound sexy." He actually sounded as if he was complaining. Or indignant.

It made her laugh. "Why in the world would I waste sexy on myself?"

"Right. You should save it for me."

"I'll be there in twenty minutes."

"I've timed the walk. It only takes ten."

"I have to change. Hanging up now, Trace."

• • •

Trace was, of course, correct. It only took ten minutes to walk to his house, and since she'd changed in under five, she got there in less than the twenty minutes she'd promised. When he opened the door, she saw lines on his face she would swear hadn't been there before, and eyes so tired looking, they wrung her heart. After a quick kiss and a long hug, she headed for the kitchen.

"I brought some herbal tea for you, to help you relax." She glanced over her shoulder as she filled the teakettle with water. "And you have to shed your jacket and tie."

"I've even been too tired to undress." But he complied. "Oh, and I was so wiped out I almost forgot what I was supposed to ask you. Emma Jacobs wants to block out time with you tomorrow to talk settlement. Is that possible?"

"Let me move a couple things around and call her. She'll be at the bank?"

"All day. On the phone with Portland when she's not trying to advise us on how to keep from stepping over some legal line or another. And, by the way, do you know what half the people wanted to talk to us about after the meeting?"

"The damages they want?"

"Wrong. They wanted to make sure we knew you had seriously reduced your hourly fee to take their case. They wanted us to pay your usual rates."

"You're not going to, are you?"

"No, we won't. We can't. We'll only pay what you billed them. But I love it that they wanted us to ignore bank policy and probably some law or other so you could get what you deserve. You didn't tell me you'd taken them on close to pro bono."

"A half dozen attorneys had already turned them down because they didn't take clients on contingency, and the ones who would take contingency cases didn't see enough money in it. I negotiated a limited contract with fees they could afford and a payment schedule that worked for them."

"And they love you for it."

When the water boiled and the tea was made, Julie suggested they take it to his bedroom where he could get undressed and satisfy her curiosity about what *he* wore to bed when she wasn't around.

It turned out to be red plaid pajamas.

She laughed as he slipped into the bottoms. "I would never have suspected you of being the plaid PJ type," she said, trying to stifle her laugh.

"My sister gave these to me for Christmas last year, I'll have you know."

"She must know you better than I do, then."

"No, she doesn't. I'm not a plaid guy. But I couldn't hurt her feelings. Besides, no one sees me in them. Well, except you now." He started to shrug on the top.

"Leave the top off and I'll rub your shoulders." She motioned him to the bed. When he lay on his back she shook her head, "How am I supposed to rub your shoulders like that? And," she continued, glancing at the obvious tenting of his pajama bottoms, "I thought you were too tired for sex."

"Apparently the relevant part decided I wasn't as soon as you were in my bedroom. Come here, beautiful." He grabbed her hands and urged her toward him.

"Wait." She shed her sweatshirt and jeans, revealing why she had gotten out of her house so quickly—she'd gone commando.

"Jesus, you've been sitting in my kitchen naked underneath those clothes?"

She straddled him and propped herself on her hands. "Not to be too technical but I believe we are all naked under our clothes, Mister Watkins."

"How about we skip the Lawyer Lady language and get to the good part."

"Which is?"

"Which is where I do this." He reversed their positions and pinned her hands beside her head. "And I do this." Lowering his head, he pressed his lips against the underside of her breasts, then teased her nipples with his tongue before backing away, kissing the sides of her breasts, the valley between them, making her squirm with the need for him to return to what she liked.

As if he knew he was tormenting her, he smiled against her breast before making the move to her nipple. "God, you taste good. Nothing I've ever had tastes as good as you do." He sipped and suckled, nipped, and licked his fill, making her heart race and her body melt.

"I thought I was here to make you feel good," she whispered.

"And you do. Just like this. Always." He skimmed his hand down her belly to her sex. "I love how wet you get when I kiss your breasts. It turns me on." He cupped her between her legs and rubbed the heel of his hand against her pubic bone before returning to her mouth, kissing her senseless, making her world spin then disappear, so all she knew was the feel of his mouth on hers and the pressure of his hand on her sex. Everything else was a blur.

Then he pulled back so he could shed his pajama pants and grab a condom from the bedside table. He was covered and back to kissing her while her mind was still groggy with the fog of desire.

Mouths crushing, tongues tangling, arms holding tight, he entered her. She moaned at the exquisite feeling of having him fill her body with his. He slowed the pace until she couldn't bear it any longer and indicated with her hips and her words how much she wanted to reach release.

The room echoed with the sound of bodies slapping together in unison, on a slick of sweat, until at last she felt her inner muscles clamp around him, and she cried out his name as he poured himself into her.

When they could breath normally again, he rolled onto the bed and went to get rid of the condom. He slipped under the sheet when he returned, and yawned. "I think you have uncovered the secret to getting me a good night's sleep."

"I'll keep it in mind the next time you're stressed out." She urged him to turn on his side, and finally had the chance to rub his shoulders. In only a few minutes she felt his body relax and his breathing change to what she knew was a sleep pattern. She moved carefully toward the edge of the bed, trying not to disturb him. But even in his sleep he must have felt her absence because he groaned a protest.

"I'm going home, Trace. I'll call you tomorrow." She pressed a kiss between his shoulder blades.

"Mmm. Love you, Juliet," he mumbled. He didn't stir or turn toward her.

Tears came to her eyes as she heard the words the first time. "I love you, too, Trace," she whispered, then slid out of bed, dressed, and bolted for home.

Chapter 20

Wednesday was another long day for Trace. He and his boss, his staff, the police, and a list of bank customers who had been victimized spent the day unraveling the details of the criminal side of what had happened. Emma and Juliet were, he knew, having a meeting mid-morning to work on the settlement side of things. He saw Emma leave, but a thumbs-up from her when she returned two hours later was the only indication of what the results were there.

What was clear was, he was going to have to spend most of his time for the foreseeable future on Clyde Lindstrom's mess, and it pissed him off.

Juliet called late in the afternoon and said how much she'd enjoyed negotiating with Emma Jacobs. She also said Emma had told her she had a job with the bank any time she wanted it. Trace held his tongue, but what went through his mind was, *Great. The woman I love gets another job offer in Portland while I'm in Ashland cleaning up after my predecessor. Nice going, Fate.*

When he got off the phone, something niggled at his mind. Something she'd said during the phone call. No, something *he'd* said. What was it?

That's it. Not something he'd said. Something he'd thought. The woman I love. That was it. Or was it? It felt like there was something more.

Maybe he had said it out loud while they were talking. No, he was sure he hadn't. He'd decided to wait until after she made her choice about Portland to tell her how he felt, so he didn't come across as putting too much pressure on her. But somehow he thought he … *Oh, shit.* Now he remembered. Before she'd left last night, she'd kissed him on the back. He'd been right on the edge of sleep, and he'd told her he loved her.

What's more, he could swear she'd said it back.

• • •

Friday was shaping up to be a rinse-and-repeat of Wednesday and Thursday. Trace was with the Portland team all day. Julie was contacting the last of her clients to get their buy-off on the settlement she and Emma Jacobs had hammered out. When she had gotten everyone's signature, she had the papers messengered to the bank, and collapsed in her chair. Done. And done.

She hadn't seen Trace on Wednesday or Thursday, although she had talked to him on the phone both evenings after he got home from very late dinners with his boss, and they'd texted like teenagers during the day. Until her clients told her they were holding a party in her honor on Friday evening, she'd planned to see him after the Portland management team had left. But there was no way she was getting out of the party. Maybe afterward she'd go see him. She had something important to tell him.

She was just wrapping up a phone call with Heather, when she walked into Martha Combes's charming old Victorian house for the party and saw Trace watching her from across the living room. It almost felt like Halloween all over again, smiling at each other across a crowded room. By the time she worked her way through the assembled collection of her clients, all of whom congratulated, hugged, or kissed her, Trace had a glass of champagne in each hand. "I thought this party was for me," she said as she took one from him.

"It is. I was invited to celebrate with you." He touched his glass to hers and took a sip.

"If she doesn't want you here, I do, handsome," Martha said as she joined them. "And I'm the hostess. So what I say goes."

"Martha, if only I didn't have such a possessive girlfriend, you and I could …" Trace let the sentence fade off into a pretend future they'd never have.

Martha snorted. "Yeah, if you didn't have a girlfriend and I didn't have forty years on you, we'd set Ashland on fire. But you do and I do, so I only get to look and enjoy."

Julie had never seen Trace blush. She enjoyed it.

Martha tapped on her champagne glass with a knife. "Ladies and gentlemen, and everyone else who's here, now that the guest of honor has arrived, let's raise our glasses to the best little lawyer in Southern Oregon. Maybe even in all Oregon." Martha turned to Julie and raised her glass. "Because of you, Julie Payne, our problem was solved and we've gotten our money back with interest. Thank you. You're the best."

To sounds of "cheers," "salud," "prost," and "l'chaim" all the glasses in the room were raised.

"Thank you, everyone. I'm touched and honored. You're the best, too." She sipped her champagne and started to say, "I can't tell you how much tonight means. It's such an …" She stopped when the phone she was still holding vibrated. Out of habit she glanced at it.

The screen said Jeff Wyatt.

"I'm sorry to do this, but I have to take this call." She put her glass on the nearest table and went out on Martha's porch.

•••

Trace knew who it was. Only one phone call could be so important that she'd take it in the middle of her victory speech. When she came back into the house, she'd be the newest deputy district attorney for Multnomah County. *Shit.*

In less than five minutes, she was back. Trace was surprised. It hadn't taken her long to make the arrangements for returning to her old office. Although maybe she'd told Jeff What's-his-name she'd call him back to work out the details. He could see from the huge smile on her face that she was happy about the new job. Happy about leaving Ashland. And him.

"So," he said, when she returned to him, "when's he want his new deputy D.A. to start?" If there was a bandage to be ripped off, he was damn well going to do it himself.

She looked surprised at the question. "End of the month, I think."

"He doesn't give you very much time to get things wrapped up here. Maybe dinner and the theater this weekend isn't such a good idea. You should probably start packing. I'll help." It killed him to do it, but if this is what she wanted, he had to support her.

She'd picked up her glass of champagne and taken a sip. "You'll help do what?"

"Pack. Like I said."

"Why would I be packing?" A funny smile played across her face. He wasn't quite sure what it meant. The smile and the comment confused him.

"To move. To Portland. For your new job. The one you just accepted."

The smile became a grin. "I don't even know if a job was about to be offered. Before he could say anything beyond hello, I told Jeff I'd thought long and hard about it and have decided to stay here."

"You decided to … why? I mean, you were so intent on making amends."

"I was. Until I realized I didn't need to. I've found whatever redemption I need here. I'm happy in Ashland doing work that matters with people who matter to me."

"When did you decide all this?"

"Tuesday evening. When I had dinner by myself and was congratulated by half the people in the restaurant for doing good work. I knew I was where I wanted to be."

"Tuesday? You decided three days ago? Exactly when were you going to tell me?"

"Tonight, after the party, I was going to drop by and do it in person. And don't look so offended. I haven't seen you since Tuesday, have I?"

"No, I guess you're right. I'm not offended. Just surprised." He touched her arm, wanting more than anything to hold her, but not sure she'd like such a blatant show of affection in front of all her clients. "This isn't because you feel like I pressured you, is it?"

"I'm not denying you're a huge part of what makes me happy here. But you didn't force me into the decision. Surely you know me well enough by now to know I'm not easily pushed. Even by you."

He gave into the urge to hold her by putting his arm around her shoulders, then bent his head and whispered for her only, "Except when I make you pray."

"Make me pray?"

He whispered even lower. "Oh, God. Oh, God. Oh, God."

She laughed, raised an eyebrow, then whispered back, "Suddenly I have this overwhelming urge to contemplate the divine. Any chance for a demonstration of your skill in helping me?"

"When the party's over, you're on." He kissed her forehead and smiled. "I love you, Juliet."

"And I love you, Romeo."

"Shakespeare couldn't have said it any better, beautiful."

More from This Author
(From *Sparked by Love* by Peggy Bird)

Leo Wilson finished fire-polishing his latest glass vessel, maneuvered it out of the heat, and with the help of his studio mate Giles Kaye, put it into an annealing oven. After the piece had been slowly brought down to room temperature, he'd inspect it and call the collector who'd commissioned the piece to come pick it up. If everything worked out, the sale would give him enough money to squeak through another month.

Leo didn't miss the scenes his ex-roommate/ex-girlfriend had thrown on a regular basis when she was working her way out of their relationship. In fact, he didn't miss much about their relationship at all. He did miss having someone to share expenses with, however. The financial pressure he'd been under for the past year or so was getting old. It was obvious he had to sell more art pieces, teach more classes, find a roommate, or take a part-time job. He wasn't sure which would present a bigger challenge—finding buyers for his work and students for his classes or finding a compatible roomie. A part-time job was possible, but that would give him less time to do his art, which meant fewer pieces to sell. But he was going to have to suck it up and pick one. Soon.

He was closing the door on the oven when Amanda St. Clair, the studio owner, called from her office. "Leo, when you have a chance, there's something here for you from the City of Vancouver."

She handed him a business-size envelope with City Hall, Vancouver, Washington as the return address when he got to her desk. "Another parking ticket?" she said. "Your visits to your buddies across the river are getting expensive."

"Luckily Vancouver's fines are a hell of a lot cheaper than Portland's. But I swear I paid the last one. And I haven't been at Firehouse Glass for a couple months." He tapped the envelope on the palm of his hand. "Besides, how did they find me here? Before, the reminders came to my house. From DMV records they got from my license plate."

"You'll never find out what the letter says by osmosis. You have to read it," Amanda said, handing him the plastic gadget she used to slice open envelopes. "And this works better than staring at it and hoping it'll pop out all by itself."

He ripped through the top of the envelope and read the enclosed letter. "Oh. My. God." Leo could barely breathe. "Oh. My. God," he repeated. "I don't fucking believe this."

"What? What?" Amanda asked.

"Read this and tell me if I'm hallucinating." He shoved the letter across the desk at her.

She scanned it then looked up, a huge smile on her face. "Oh, my God, is right, Leo! You got the commission." She yelled, "Giles, come here. Quick."

Giles stuck his head into the office. "What's going on? Did one of you win the lottery or something?"

"Close," Amanda said, handing him the letter. "Look, Leo landed the grant from Vancouver."

"The $75,000 one?"

"The very one."

Although Leo hadn't taken his eyes off the letter Giles had returned to the desk, he didn't need to see her to hear the pride in Amanda's voice. His mother wouldn't sound any prouder at the news.

"Congratulations, Leo," Giles said. "This is great." He clapped his colleague on the back but Leo didn't respond. "Hey, did we lose you? Are you still on this planet?"

"Not sure," Leo croaked then cleared his throat. "I never thought this would happen." He picked up the letter, re-reading it, still not sure he believed the words. "This was such a long shot. I figured my idea was too out there. But, look, they said … ah … where is it?" He ran his finger down the letter to the sentence he was looking for. "Here it is. 'Your design is bold, creative, and in the spirit of the region's arts as well as our annual celebration of Independence Day.'"

He didn't know which to be happy about first—having his art respected or having the financial picture he'd just been worrying about dramatically improved. For the moment, he decided to go with enjoying this chance to exhibit his art—he'd celebrate the money when he saw the first check.

"I'm going to have an art installation millions of people will see," he said.

"The number's more like tens of thousands," Giles said, "but for sure you'll get attention from the media. They always cover the fireworks at Fort Vancouver like a blanket. Biggest news story every Fourth of July."

"Don't rain on my parade, Giles. I've never landed anything like this before, and if I want to think there will be millions of people there, let me," Leo said.

"Well, there'll be a hell of a traffic jam on the I-5 Bridge if you're right. But you'll need more than congratulations to make this happen. If I recall the proposal, it's pretty complicated. What can I do to help you?"

"Yes, Leo, what do you need from the studio and from us?" Amanda asked.

"Give me a chance to absorb the news and we'll talk," he responded.

Leo made a quick phone call to the Clark County Arts Commission chair, whose name was on the letter, to officially accept the commission and make arrangements for all the paperwork he needed to fill out. Then he took his studio mates up on their offer to strategize. The three artists spent most of the morning planning how to get Leo's project accomplished. Specifically, how much could be done at the GlassCo studio and how much would have to be done in Vancouver, with his buddies at Firehouse Glass.

It was, as Giles had said, a complicated endeavor. Leo had proposed a large art installation on the grounds of the Historic Reserve where each year, the city of Vancouver, Washington, sponsored a huge party to celebrate the Fourth of July. There was music, art, and entertainment, food vendors and space to stroll around the grounds of an old army fort, now managed by the city. After dark, what was billed as the largest pyrotechnic display west of the Mississippi lit up the night sky. The fireworks could be heard, if not seen, all over the city as well as from the boats on the Columbia River and many parts of Portland, Oregon, which was right across the river from Vancouver.

The display had inspired Leo's proposal. Instead of a static, in-one-place exhibit of glass, he designed large and small glass fireworks to be installed in the trees and structures around the former parade grounds of the base where the crowds picnicked while they waited for the after-dark fireworks display.

Each burst would be made of slender tubes of glass in various sizes, shapes, and colors and would require careful installation to connect the pieces in the correct manner and secure them into place. Floodlit from below, Leo's fireworks would "go off" all evening as a computer controlling the lights would turn them off and on to simulate the moment when the shells burst into spectacular designs in the sky.

The project was large. It was complicated. It was expensive. And it was what Leo hoped would get his work the attention he'd been struggling for his whole career.

All he had to do was get a couple permits from the City of Vancouver, and he would be on his way. How hard could it be to get a couple of permits?

• • •

Three months later, Leo was at Firehouse Glass in Vancouver where he was creating some of the pieces for the display. The only official paper he had from the City of Vancouver were more parking tickets from his hours of working with his glass blower friends and forgetting to plug the meter.

Today they'd gotten the last of the pieces for one of the smaller fireworks completed and had spent the time they were working sympathizing with Leo about his difficulty getting the appropriate permissions.

"I mean, it's not like I'm misting the crowds with toxic waste, or endangering salmon or something. All I want to do is put up an art installation," he griped as he brought a gather of glass out of the glory hole. His attention was diverted to the job at hand for the next bit of time, but when the piece was shaped and in the kiln, he returned to his venting about the city.

"Have you guys had trouble with them about permits and things?" he asked.

Frank Steward, a longtime friend and colleague, shook his head. "No, but then we've never done anything more complex than be part of a team putting up a piece of public art in a city park. It's more complicated in the Reserve. Part of the property is managed by the city and there's National Park land involved in the visitor center and down near the recreated old fort. And there's a trust involved somehow, but I'm not sure how. It's kind of a special deal."

"Yeah, well, maybe if I'd known how difficult it would be to get the damn permits, I'd have thought twice about submitting

169

my proposal," Leo said. "This woman who works for the city, this Shannon Morgan, is driving me nuts. She's supposed to be helping me get this done, but she puts up hurdles to keep me from accomplishing anything faster than I can jump over them. Everything I propose gets one of two responses: "no" or "not possible." They're the only words she knows. So far, she's turned down my request for some help from the city to install the glass, refused to get me a permit for the lighting, isn't sure if I can have access to the site early in the week before the Fourth to get the pieces up, and she's wavering about letting me use some of the sites I picked out but won't tell me why. She's a pain in the butt."

"Have you talked to her?"

"Of course I've talked to her. At least weekly for three months." Leo was indignant Frank would think he hadn't pursued this vigorously.

"I know you've *communicated* with her. I meant have you *talked* to her. You know, used your legendary skills with women to persuade her. Up close and in person." His buddy leered at him.

"Yeah, right. Legendary skills. You mean the ones getting rusty from lack of use since Cathy bailed on me?" Leo pursed his mouth and frowned. "But you might have hit on something. If I can't convince her with logic on the phone and in email, maybe I can dazzle her with bullshit in person. I've always had luck impressing the mothers of the women I date so maybe … "

"How do you know she's your mother's age?"

"I don't know for sure. But she fusses at what I want to do and tries to tell me what I can't do like my mom does. I mean, I already have one mother, and I love her. If I need a lecture, I can call her. I don't need a city employee filling in for her."

"Make an appointment with this Shannon Morgan. Show her what you're doing. Buy her lunch or something. Butter her up. Maybe you can soften her crustiness."

Leo thought about his friend's suggestion for a minute. "You're right. I need to see this woman in person to size her up. But no appointment. I want the element of surprise on my side. I'll go over to city hall right now. I have the design specs in the truck. I've got images on my phone of some of my other installations. I'll show her what I'm doing and see if it makes a difference."

For more great novels from Peggy Bird, check out her Second Chances series:

Beginning Again

Praise for *Beginning Again*:
"Both Liz and Collins are great characters. Liz is not a bitter middle aged woman, but instead a very strong and brave lady. I really enjoyed *Beginning Again* because it was an easy read that made my gray autumn day a little bit less gray." —Long & Short Reviews

Loving Again

Together Again

Praise for *Together Again*:
"…a very enjoyable romance. I loved the main characters and the great writing. I always admire strong, independent women, so if you also enjoy those qualities in a heroine, and enjoy a well-written romance, I recommend this one." —Night Owl Reviews

Trusting Again

Praise for *Trusting Again*:
"The book moves along at a nice pace and the characters are believable and realistic. It is a well-written story with a wonderful ending!" —Harlequin Junkie

Believing Again

Falling Again

In the mood for more Crimson Romance?
Check out *Forgiving Jackson by Alicia Hunter Pace* at
CrimsonRomance.com.

www.ingramcontent.com/pod-product-compliance
Lightning Source LLC
Chambersburg PA
CBHW010311100726
47905CB00011B/3294